WILLIAM'S WISHES

JENNIFER LYNCH

Republished June 2022

Jennifer Lynch has asserted her right under the Copyright Design and Patents Act 1988 to be identified as the author of this work
This book is a work of fiction, names and characters are a product of the author's imagination and any resemblance to actual persons living, or dead is entirely coincidental.
This book is sold subject to the condition that it shall not, by way of trade or otherwise be lent, re-sold, hired out or otherwise circulated without the publisher's prior written consent in any form of binding or cover other than which it is published.
Published by Jennifer Lynch
copyright Jennifer Lynch 2012

DEDICATION

I dedicate this book to all the mothers of adopted children and to all the birth mothers who were forced to leave their children behind.

William's Wishes							Jennifer Lynch

CHAPTER 1
REBECCA

Sister, Sister, don't pick up the babies, they need to stop crying. There are far too many to cope with,' declared the Reverend Mother. Mary was used to Margaret being sharp, she was frequently hard to work with, but surely the woman had a heart?

'We can't leave them crying all night,' Mary replied, but she knew it was a waste of time explaining anything to Margaret when she constantly repeated, attachment always caused problems. She was right, whenever they had become involved, it had always ended in tears. It was natural to feel sad when the babies were taken away from their mothers, the girls were distraught, but over the years Mary had learned that nothing changed at St. Catherine's. When the paperwork was complete and the adoptions arranged, it was a cruel world for these young women. Hopefully, without the burden of a child to care for, they would soon return to a 'normal life.'

Mary wondered what 'normal was,' over the years, she'd learned to accept her situation and she was grateful but as she tugged at the side of a heavy cot, she knew how these women felt. The cots were rusty, unhygienic but they were secure. They were all they could afford, with so little funding. Wooden cots had been about for years, but they were way too expensive for these babies, the unwanted ones, Margaret thought it was unnecessary to change them, so they made do.

'Sister, if the babies cry in the night, they will have to be fed, once every four hours is enough. I've written their feed times down on the wall chart to make it easier for you. If they're too much for you, hand them back to their mothers, they can be woken. We are too busy for all the night feeds. We also need to get Rebecca's baby ready for adoption in the morning, so please pack her clothes, We can only spare one set and a couple of nappies for the journey, as usual. You'll also have to make up some formula milk to take with you. As Margaret moved towards the door, she appeared to carry the whole world on her shoulders. The years had been unkind to her. She seldom smiled. Margaret had worked at St Catherine's for nearly fifty years. During that time, she must have experienced changes in attitude towards unmarried mothers she thought, but here at St. Catherine's views remained much the same. The furnishings were form the thirties and the home was in desperate need of updating. Margaret was proud of her personal contribution, but Mary often wondered if the donations could have been better spent. It was different for her because her work had been emotionally challenging, each baby that left, was a reminder of the child she herself had lost. The child for which she was punished.

After a very long and painful labour, Mary gave birth to a stillborn child, after which she was given the choice of being sent into a convent or working at St. Catherine's. Mary decided to stay and take a job that was eventually to become her life's work, helping the mothers' part with their children. She had learned to accept the role because it meant a better future for these young women. In doing so, she'd experienced many heart-rendering moments. As for her own family, she'd tried to keep in touch, but her parents had made it clear years ago, that they didn't want to correspond with her. When her mother discovered her pregnancy, it was easier for her to pretend her daughter was dead. She told people she died of illness she'd contracted nursing the soldiers during the war. Her parent's lies were beyond comprehension. Margaret explained that most people believed she was dead, and that's why she never received letters. Mary found it hard to believe that none of her family or friends wrote, but Margaret was privy to many secrets, and she thought it unwise to push it any further. St. Catherine's was run with a rod of iron and Margaret didn't share her secrets.

CHAPTER 2

1940

It was 1940 and not long into the Second World War when Mary met William. She was only nineteen years of age, but they were in love. Sadly, very soon after they met, Mary received the news that William was going to France to fight the Germans. It was a shock for both of them because he'd not long signed up, and they doubted that he'd be sent so quickly. Mary was horrified by the news and terrified at the thought of losing him. She would wait for him, however long he was away, because when he eventually came home, they would marry.

The night before William left for France, he gave her a beautiful ring. Mary was thrilled. Unfortunately, William never came home, as was the case with many brave young pilots during the war. Mary made a promise to herself that her love would never be forgotten. When some weeks later, she discovered she was carrying his baby, she knew the child would be a constant reminder of their love and her tragic loss. Unfortunately, the moment her family found out about her pregnancy, everything changed. They didn't understand why she hadn't waited until William came home and they'd married. Mary was considered foolish and unworthy of their love. She very quickly realised her life would never be the same again. Her family had abandoned her and St. Catherine's very soon became her future. The other options were inconceivable.

CHAPTER 3
REBECCA'S BABY

Just sign the papers, Rebecca. The longer you leave it, the harder it will be. If you don't sign now, you won't be able to return home. You're one of the lucky ones. Many girls, don't return to their parents. Jane is going back to her flat in East London, on her own,' said, the Reverend Mother.

Rebecca took a quick look at Jane. Her back was turned. She appeared to be sleeping, but she was crying. She heard her sobbing in the night, and it didn't look like she had moved since then. Jane had given up eating and she only drank because the nuns insisted that unless she did, she wouldn't be allowed home. They warned her that they'd have to send for the doctor to give her another examination. 'You won't be allowed home unless you are strong enough,' they repeated.

Rebecca was sick of their threats! If they say that to me, I'll walk out, she thought but her body was weak, and she was still breastfeeding. Why did they force her to do that? Why did she see her baby, it just made things harder! What was the point when she'd been told she couldn't keep her? It was slow torture and it needed to end!

'I don't want to see my baby' she'd shouted, immediately after the birth, but it was too late, once Bridgette was born and the afterbirth removed, she glanced across and saw her child wrapped in a large white cloth and her heart told her, she had to hold her. The feeling was overwhelming.

'Are you sure? If you don't want to bond with your baby, we can take her away now and you won't have to breastfeed her. If you hold her, you will be responsible for her feeds,' she was told.

'Please, bring her here,' Rebecca demanded.

Bridgette was without doubt, the most beautiful baby Rebecca had ever seen, a miniature her. Her heart and soul were in her child, along with her breath and blood. She was the miracle that she alone had kept alive for nine whole months. Rebecca had screamed and asked for more gas and air during a difficult labour, but the pain had turned from agony to a flow of love which joined them together. A bond which couldn't be broken, the connection of mother and daughter.

'If I sign my name, will I ever see my baby, again?' asked Rebecca.

'No, you won't. You know that, we explained that from the start,' replied, Mary.

'But I didn't know I would feel this way,' cried Rebecca.

'I'm afraid your feelings don't come into it. We have to put the child first,' Mary replied sharply.

'There are families that are more suitable, waiting for babies. You do want the best for your child, don't you?' asked Mary. A tear started to form in Mary's eye which she quickly wiped away. She felt compassion for Rebecca, but she'd learned how to hide her feelings after so many emotional partings.

Rebecca looked over to the doorway to see if she could catch a glimpse of Bridgette, but she'd become a muffled cry, along with the other twenty or so babies. Bridgette was now a statistic, mother unmarried; father unknown.

CHAPTER 4
LETTING GO

The bus jolted from side to side along country roads and Rebecca fingered her bus ticket. It was an hour's journey to the city. Was she having a bad dream? It was the worst nightmare she'd ever had! She knew this day would come, but so soon! Wrapped tightly in a shawl, cradled in her arms, was Bridgette. Bridgette, why had she called her that? It was the name she'd wanted to be called, but she couldn't remember why.

What will happen to little Bridgette after today? Rebecca could feel the warmth from her baby's body resting on her lap as she quietly observed her breathing. Does anyone know why I'm on this bus, the number 46 to Westminster, she thought angrily. If these people see me, later, won't they wonder where she's gone? Maybe they'll think she wasn't mine. I was just looking after her, but they're wrong because Bridgette will always be mine. Wherever she goes and whatever happens to her, we'll always be part of each other.

Rebecca looked out of the window. It had started to drizzle. Raindrops fell down the windows, and her finger began to trace the droplets like a child. Which one will finish its journey and what happens to the lost raindrops? They're like me. I'm a lost raindrop.

'I want to get off at the next stop; driver,' she shouted, as she suddenly realised their location.

'The next stop, Miss, yeah, course.'

Rebecca waited until the bus stopped before struggling off with a heavy bag over one arm and her child resting on the other. She didn't want to fall. The massive step down caused her to wobble because her body was still weak.

Rebecca had been at Catherine's Maternity home for almost two months after being admitted full term! Some girls went in early, the ones who found it hard to cope. Rebecca hoped it would all go away until she was forced to face reality, following an appointment with the midwife.

'Don't be silly,' she had said. 'You can't possibly go through this on your own. You need to think about the health of both you and the baby and prepare.'

The streets of London were crowded today and dust flew into her face from passing traffic. Rebecca kept the shawl tightly wrapped around Bridgette. She was unable to look at her watch but she guessed it must be lunchtime because men in business suits walked rapidly in and out of cafes. Her eyes caught a glimpse of Big Ben, it was quarter past one. She had a quarter of an hour to take the short walk to Banbury Street and find the head office of the Adoption Society. She'd forgotten the name of the social worker because her mind had gone blank. How was she expected to remember anything at a time like this?

Baby Bridgette started to wake. Rebecca knew she would soon be asking for her bottle and she decided to quicken her pace. Her heart beat fast as she discovered the name of the road affixed to the side of a building. She wanted to go back to the bus, to travel anywhere as long as it was away from London. I can't do this, she thought with tears streaming down her face.

Rebecca remembered her parents and brother in Ireland. It would be difficult to return home with a baby in tow. She would never be allowed to see them. This is no good. I can't go through with this. It doesn't feel right, her head screamed, but her feet were still walking. What choice did she have, but to carry on?

Mrs Neave stood in the doorway of number 12 Banbury Street. You must be Rebecca,' she asked kindly.

'Yes, Madam' answered Rebecca in a small voice

'And this is?' asked Mrs Neave in a demanding tone.

'Bridgette.'

'Bridgette, we have a lot of Bridgette's. Do come this way quickly, my dear because we haven't a lot of time.'

Mrs Neave led Rebecca into a large room containing an old leather sofa and some comfortable chairs. Everything in the room smelt of polish, the couch, the furniture and the walls which were made of wood panels. The floor was tiled and highly glossed. There was a copy of the Times on the edge of the sofa. Who would read a newspaper at a time like this, thought Rebecca as she pushed it aside?

'Now dear, I will take down the last few details as we have to complete a report on ... Bridgette. Then, I'll hold her while you sort out your things. Would that be all right?' asked Mrs Neave, in an empathic tone.

Rebecca sensed that Mrs Neave was slightly more caring than anticipated, but she found it hard to speak. When there was no reply from Rebecca, Mrs Neave continued to talk, taking no notice.

'When did you last feed Bridgette?'

Rebecca's mind turned over and over. Her throat felt parched, and words were impossible. She was also finding it hard to breathe and started to cough.

'I'll get you a glass of water dear, I know it's difficult, but in time you will understand it was for the best. You'll soon carry on with your life and make a fresh start, and who knows, you may get married and have more children. Your baby's going to a perfect home. Mr and Mrs Woods are coming this afternoon to fetch Bridgette on trial adoption. They are excellent parents. They already have one little girl who badly wants a sister. So, you see Rebecca, Bridgette, will be very well cared for. Her parents are qualified teachers, so think what they can teach her. She'll have opportunities that she couldn't have with you!

Rebecca laid Bridgette down on the leather sofa and took a large sip of water. Some of the water dripped on to the couch. Her hands were shaking. How could she let another woman hold her child? She felt angry that Bridgette would never know her. She had only ever lost animals; how could this compare? When she lost her dog, Toby, at twelve years old, she'd cried for weeks.? Would her child feel dead, like Toby?

Twenty minutes later, Rebecca walked towards the bus stop in a complete daze, and the bus had just left. Could things get any worse she muttered? If it's going to rain, I want to get soaked so I can feel something. I want the rain to let me know I'm still alive because I'm dead inside. My daughter has gone. Someone, please listen to me. You, over there, waiting for the bus, my daughter has gone. They took her away and now I'm lost!

When Rebecca finally arrived at her flat in the late afternoon. It felt cold. There had been little sun all day, and it was more like autumn, which was odd for the end of August. Her mind kept churning over 'when you go home to your parents.' The lies they told. They knew I was going back to my flat. Perhaps that was the story they gave Mr and Mrs Woods, to make them feel better. I'm never going home to my parents. I couldn't go back even if I wanted too because I haven't enough money. Anyway, this is my home, but it doesn't feel like it. It's just an empty shell.

Rebecca looked at the electric meter; it was low. It should last until the end of the week with a bit of luck. She hoped to return to work by then. She'd been told to stay off for another month, but how could she when she was running out of money. She walked over to the refrigerator. A bottle of milk which smelt vile, was standing inside the door. Its odour had taken over the whole fridge. Rebecca removed it and filled it up with hot water from the kettle. She had no idea why! No more warming bottles, or breastfeeding, she thought, at least I won't have to do that. She moved wearily over to her usual chair, which was next to an open fireplace. She often lit a fire in the colder months. I'll do that later when I've had a little rest. It will brighten the place up a bit, she muttered. Five minutes later, she was asleep.

Rebecca woke in the early hours of the morning. The flat smelt musty, and it was cold. She still held an empty mug in her hand from the night before, and her head was pounding. For a few minutes, Rebecca didn't know where she was. Then to her horror, she remembered what had taken place the day before. Rebecca thought about her baby's shawl resting against her skin. She could see Bridgette's eyes looking up at her just before she handed her to Mrs Neave. The worse thing of all, was, her baby's smell lingered as a reminder of the horror she'd experienced.

Rebecca took a long deep breath and tried to rid herself of the painful memory, but it was impossible.

She knew that she'd never again touch Bridgette's tiny hands, grip her finger, look into her eyes or imagine her as a grown-up. She was no longer part of her life, and it wasn't right to think about her future. Only emptiness remained, as Rebecca struggled with the reality of what had happened. It was a chapter of her life that she wanted to close for good. I have to make changes, she thought. I can't be weak Rebecca, I need to be someone else, an entirely different person. She strode decisively to her wardrobe, which contained dresses that she hadn't had the opportunity to wear.

A year ago, she had met a very wealthy lady who befriended her. The lady had since moved away to live abroad because the English weather had not been kind to her arthritis which in recent years was chronic. When Iris left, she left a big bag of clothes for Rebecca. 'You'll wear them one day, keep them. I have no use for them now, and besides, the colours suit you,' she'd said, handing them over. Iris wanted to move on with her life, so the clothes had to go!

'I'll make a new start,' Bridgette said out loud, hoping that someone would acknowledge her. Iris's clothes still hung at one end of her wardrobe. She hadn't looked at them since she left because of her pregnancy. There appeared to be a stylish trouser suit. It was out of fashion because the legs were narrow and the full trouser leg was trendy, but despite that, it still held possibilities. Perhaps with a necktie, thought Rebecca, as she slung it over her bed. She wasn't up to trying on clothes on right now.

Mustering up the energy to do anything felt impossible but seeing the clothes had lifted her.

Rebecca's flat consisted of one small room on the bottom floor of an old Georgian house in East London. Her furniture was scarce; a single bed, an old chest of drawers, a bedside cabinet and a single armchair. There was also a square oak dining table, which fitted nicely in the bay window. Usually, Rebecca would put flowers in a glass vase in the centre of the table, which always looked cheerful. Today, the place appeared dingy. It wasn't neglected, but it needed a really good airing because she hadn't been there for two months.

She gazed out of the window to the street below. It was getting light, and the sky had turned from deep indigo to various shades of pink and mauve. Grey clouds were scattered in between which created a mysterious look with the rising sun in the distance.

Rebecca wondered about her co-workers in the factory. What would they say to her now? When she'd spoken to the girls at work about her dilemma, a few of them felt sorry for her, but many stopped talking. Previously, everyone said 'good morning' or 'goodnight', even if they didn't know her but, as her pregnancy progressed, she didn't hear any friendly greetings. She just noticed them surveying her body without acknowledgement. She had quickly turned from a young, slim, desirable woman, to someone entirely different.

Along with Rebecca's feelings of neglect, she had also suffered from morning sickness, that seemed to go on forever. Looking back, she realised that this phase only lasted for about three months, but at the time it felt like forever. She had pretended to need the toilet so she could splash her face with cold water which helped a little. But the worst thing about working through her pregnancy was, she still had to face Michael, the man with his fancy suit and a brand-new car. Him, the man who pretended not to know her when he knew damn well, he did, and intimately. Michael, how often had she cried his name? Night after night, with tears rolling down her cheeks, soaking her pillow until she finally drifted off. How could he have said those things and not meant any of them? He'd let her down, badly.

One cold morning in February, she'd made the mistake of telling her colleague Eileen about her secret meetings with Michael.

'Holy Mary, didn't your mother ever tell you, never mess with a married man!'

'He told me he wasn't married, he's separated' replied Rebecca in a whisper, feeling a little ashamed.

'He wears a wedding ring on his finger, that's married in my book,' replied Eileen. There was no doubt in her mind that Rebecca was wasting her time. It was unfortunate, and she felt some empathy towards the girl, but at the same time it was apparent that she'd behaved stupidly. What was she thinking of going after the boss? She must have lost her mind.

'Michael told me that he'd already left her. We were planning on starting a new life together. He was looking for a place for us to live. I wasn't allowed to tell anyone about us until it was all arranged.'

Tears of frustration streamed down Rebecca's face. She was devastated because Michael had rejected her, and at the same time she was frightened by the predicament he'd left her in. She felt lonely, isolated and desperate, and her only friend didn't appear to care.

'Did you really think he'd leave his wife? Why would he leave his good life to be with a penniless Irish shrimp-like you?' Eileen's words were harsh, but Rebecca knew they carried the truth. Thinking back, she realised what a fool she'd been. Why, oh why had she been taken in by him? Was it his charm, good looks, or, was it that he was in a position of power, that drew her in? Whatever the reason, it was far too late now to waste time any time thinking about.

Rebecca bit back the tears but was engulfed by a heavy feeling in her chest. She remembered that she'd told Eileen how she loved Michael, but she'd turned sharply away in disgust. She didn't want to listen. She had to get back to work. Rebecca had slowly followed her back to the factory. Their tea break was over, they only had ten minutes, which was always a rush. Rebecca had picked up the cigarettes and shoved them into their boxes. They were meant to make sure they were all the right way up, but why should she? I love him, she thought naively, and his wife doesn't care about him.

How could she have been that stupid? She went to pick up her coat. The paper shop would be open soon, and she wanted to buy a newspaper.

Sometime later, Rebecca returned to her flat, with the paper under her arm and placed it on the table to read. She then picked up the photo of Michael in a small round brass frame. She loved this photograph. He'd told her it was taken years ago long before he met his wife Jane, but she wasn't convinced. Had anything that Michael said, been real? 'There's no point in hanging onto ghosts, she thought as she hurled his picture into the bin. It would only remind her of the past.

Rebecca walked over to the fire, it didn't take her long to start a roaring blaze with a few bits of kindling and the remainder of a coal scuttle. She would have to be careful because it was the last of the coal, and things would be hard until she found another job. It wasn't possible to return to the cigarette factory. She couldn't face the girls, or standing in a line filling packets until five-thirty! How she hated that clock. The cigarettes also made marks on people's fingers. It was intolerable. Most of the girls smoked; it went with the territory. When people smelt her clothes, they assumed that she too was a heavy smoker because the smell would never go away. Smoking was a filthy habit, but she had never felt as dirty as she did right now.

Rebecca went into the bathroom and ran a warm deep bath and soaked herself. I'll scrub myself clean of everything that has ever happened to me, she declared. When I'm properly clean, I can start afresh. I'll put on some of those smart clothes and get as far away from here as possible. No-one will remember Rebecca from the cigarette factory.

CHAPTER 5
BRIDGETTE

Bridgette stood in her party dress, today she was seven. The dress was made of white chiffon with multiple petticoats and rows of lace. The skirt which came just above her knees flared out due. She'd been told it wasn't new. It had belonged to another child, but it hadn't been worn much. Bridgette loved the dress. She was used to hand-me-downs. Her parents weren't wealthy, and new things were old things, that had been cleaned, or adjusted. Many of her clothes had been worn by her older sister. Bridgette loved the dress, and she'd never seen it on her sister, so she was very excited to wear it to the party.

Bridgette school friends were coming to her house today, she'd invited the whole class! When her mother asked who did she wanted to invite, she was unsure because it was hard to decide who her real friends were. Bridgette wasn't sure if anyone liked her, but her logical mind told her that they must do, or they wouldn't play with her. So, she decided the best thing would be to invite all the girls, then no one would be left out. At the back of her mind though, Bridgette was worried about becoming upset. It was her special day when she was old enough to go to church and take communion with her mother. Bridgette knew that being seven was very important in the Catholic Church, and she was enjoying that feeling of importance, but she also had a secret that she didn't want anyone to share.

'Be careful you don't get mud on that dress playing in the garden. It will get filthy being white,' warned her mother. She realised that her friends wouldn't be arriving for a while and she wanted to try out her new bike.

'I'll try not to,' shouted Bridgette confidently, but she knew her mother was right, playing in the garden in a white dress before her friends arrived was risky!

It was a beautiful day. The sun was shining, and the sky was cloudless as the girls arrived in their party dresses. At least the weather is good thought Bridgette, but she was still anxious about them mentioning she was adopted. She had told a few of the girls at school in the last few weeks, and she felt guilty. Bridgette didn't want her mother to know because she felt as if she'd betrayed a family secret.

Her present sat on the lawn, and it looked beautiful. It was a large tricycle which had been painted blue and white by her father. It was made from metal, with huge wheels. It glistened in the sun. Some of the other girls were already riding two-wheeler bikes so Bridgette felt a bit silly, and wondered if the girls would think she was a baby. But she couldn't help but adore this tricycle, what it didn't have in speed, it made up for in style! Bridgette suddenly felt proud that her father had restored the trike. It wasn't babyish, it was unique!

Dawn suddenly ran over to the tricycle.

'Wow, what a huge trike, I've never seen one as big as this before. Can I have a go?'

Great, thought Bridgette, they like it, and she started to relax and have fun. As long as her friends enjoyed the party, she would be popular. To Bridgette's amazement, the girls all took turns to ride the trike around the garden while the others followed behind chasing and laughing. The bike went much faster than Bridgette anticipated. The girls finally finished pushing it around because they were worn out but everyone looked as if they were having fun.

'I think your trike is really great. I wish I had one', said Gillian.

Exhausted, and with everyone beginning to dirty their party dresses, Bridgette led the way into the lounge where her mother had arranged for them to play pass the parcel. Her mother then played a tune on the piano, and when she stopped playing, a layer of brown paper was taken off. There were sweets hidden in between the layers of paper. Bridgette suddenly felt proud of her Mum. This party was going to be good, and thankfully no-one was in the least bit interested in mentioning the word, adopted.

CHAPTER 6
SCHOOL

Bridgette stood alone in the playground while watching the other children play tag. Her sister was playing jacks with some girls she didn't know. Fiona was good at jacks. It involved bouncing a tiny bouncy ball with one hand and picking up pieces of metal in between the bounces. The jacks were metal star shaped pieces that you could grasp in your hand. Bridgette wasn't good at jacks, or any ball games. She hated being out in the playground, where everyone was running around shouting and pushing each other, so she seldom joined in. She was scared of being called stupid. Bridgette tried once or twice to play but found it impossible because the ball kept rolling away. In the end, the other girls became impatient with her, so she walked off. Why was it so difficult? She'd tried and tried and had even practiced at home, but it didn't make any difference! Once she joined in with the skipping, but the rope was going too fast for her, 'one, two, three and jump in', shouted the girls. One, two, three and Bridgette couldn't move because she was afraid of making a fool of herself! She couldn't keep up with the other girls, so she'd let them down. If Bridgette managed to jump in, she was soon gasping for air. It was too much physical effort and she had chest problems.

Navesmere was Bridgette's second school. Her parents had moved her from her first school because she was unhappy. She liked her new school and had started to make friends. Recently, she'd met Diane. Diane wasn't like the others because she spent a lot of time on her own. She didn't join in with the games either and Bridgette often found her on her own in an empty classroom at playtime.

One day, Bridgette was sitting in a classroom when Diane approached her. Diane was well-liked by the other girls because despite being a loner, she was confident. She was also double-jointed and did incredible things with her fingers and thumbs, which made her popular with her classmates who often sat watching her, saying things like 'that's impossible, please can you show me how to do it!' Most of the time, she had a massive crowd of friends around her so Bridgette couldn't speak to her but today Diane wanted to talk to her.

'I hear that your adopted,' asked Diane, as she moved closer to Bridgette.

'Yes, I am, but who told you?' Bridgette asked, wondering how she found out.

Oh, I don't remember now. I'm adopted too. My real mother lives in a town not far away, she has written to us. She didn't want to give me away, and wants to see me now. My mother says she's a sort of relative.'

Bridgette's mind couldn't fathom this out. She thought when you were adopted, you never found out who your real mother was, let alone meet her. Her young mind was beginning to realise that there were different situations and, although Diane was adopted, it didn't sound the same as her story. This was confusing, and perhaps she was lying? It was better not to ask questions.

Bridgette then decided to tell Diane her own story.

'I arrived by train. I was wearing woolen baby clothes, and it was boiling. I think my Mum and Dad went to London to get me,' she said suddenly, repeating the words her mother had told her. Unfortunately, Diane had already lost interest in her story, because her friends had appeared, and once again she was playing with her joints!

CHAPTER 7
TEN YEARS LATER

Bridgette was seventeen, young, pretty, with brown shoulder-length hair and piercing bright blue eyes. Her boss had just taken a photograph of her because he was using up some film in his camera. She liked Trevor, if only he were younger. She wanted to marry a man like him. He was severe most of the time, but he still wanted to have fun. They had some great office outings together, which was brilliant because it made her feel part of a team.

Bridgette operated a busy switchboard and looked after the reception area, seeing clients politely in and out of the office. At first, it was really frightening having full responsibility for all the callers because she worried that she might cut someone off or write a number down incorrectly. However, after a few weeks, things had become clearer, and Bridgette had started to settle into her job, except for one bad day when, one her bosses roared like a lion at her for losing a caller. She really enjoyed her work. Bridgette also liked being on the front desk because people always talked to her and she looked forward to seeing their familiar faces.

The Solicitors' offices were spread over three floors, which meant that quite a few clients had to climb two flights of stairs for their appointments. Most of the time, the solicitors would come down to greet their clients, which Bridgette thought was polite and stopped them from moaning at her! Gordon's wife had come in today. She often stopped to chat with the girls in the office before she went shopping in the town. She frequently went into the shopping centre, and she popped by to unload her shopping into her husband's car, so she wouldn't have to carry it home. The couple lived just a short distance from the town and from what Bridgette understood, in a beautiful house. Bridgette thought that Angela was glamorous with a great taste in fashion. Angela was in her mid-thirties. Her hair was short, blonde and cut in an elegant style and she appeared to wear designer clothes. She also had a very petite figure, with a somewhat domineering personality, which didn't go unnoticed. The girls in the office frequently discussed Angela's life. They liked to gossip and Bridgette often heard more than she wanted to!

Gordon was a hen-pecked husband, who tried his best to do everything he could for his wife, from supplying her with money to purchase the latest fashions, to buying some costly additions for their beautiful house. Sometimes, Gordon would spill the beans and tell his secretary about his frustrations.

'What on earth does she want, now?' he'd say, despairingly!

It seemed that whatever Gordon gave to Angela, to cheer her up, it never seemed to work. However, there was one thing the couple wanted more than anything else in the world, and that was a child. Bridgette had heard the stories of Angela's health problem. She'd had various operations to make it easier to conceive, but sadly it didn't make any difference. The chances of them having their own child were extremely slim. The more anxious Angela became, the harder it was to conceive. Bridgette heard mutterings of the word 'adoption', but she'd been told that the adoption process was very different from the time she was adopted. It was now virtually impossible to adopt a baby because there were so few. Partly, due to abortions.

Today, like many other days, Bridgette was trying to get on with her work which involved answering the switchboard, which was extremely busy, and finding the time to type out documents, a juggling act that she'd got used over the past six months, when suddenly Angela approached her and began to ask her questions, in rapid succession.

'What's it like being adopted, Bridgette, does it bother you? How old were you? Do you want to trace your real mother? What does she know about you? Do you get upset when people talk about it?'

Bridgette sat gazing at this woman. A woman who had everything except a child. She drew in a long deep breath, which one should she answer first? She was so busy, and it wasn't the right time to have this conversation. Angela's persistent questions irritated her. She was the boss's wife but surely that didn't give her the right to stick her nose into her personal life. She decided to tell her how she felt, as quickly as she could, so she'd be left alone to finish her work.

'Being adopted is complicated. I don't mind it, because it is something that I've grown up with and I do want to trace my natural mother, one day. I understand that you have to be eighteen and I'm not eighteen yet,' she replied, hoping that this would be the end of the conversation.

Angela continued to barrage her with questions. She wanted to know exactly when she was adopted and what her parents told her.

'I've always known. I think that it's the best way. My mum and dad used to tell me a little story about how I arrived on a train in woolen baby clothes and I had a red face because it was a scorching day. Apparently, I had eczema, which soon got better after I had been staying with them for a few weeks,' Bridgette blurted out all in one breath.

Angela looked satisfied; at least it had silenced her for a little while. Please don't do that to me again, thought Bridgette. I don't know if I can handle divulging so much about myself. Yet, she felt a little sorry for Angela. It was awful that the couple couldn't have their own children.

Gordon and Angela waited months for Johnny to arrive. Bridgette still worked in the solicitor's office, but now, she'd been promoted to legal secretary. She was told that Gordon and Angela weren't able to adopt a baby, but they were allowed to adopt a two-year-old.

A few weeks later, Bridgette gazed out of the office window. She had been typing for hours, and it was time for a cup of coffee. She walked over to the coffee machine. It was a little strong, but it kept her going all day. Down in the car park below, Bridgette could see Angela. She held a large pack of nappies in one hand, which she was putting in the boot of Gordon's Mercedes. Her other hand was occupied with a small child who Bridgette assumed must be Johnny. The little boy looked happy trotting alongside his mother, and she carried him down the steps, which led to the ground floor of the old Georgian building. Bridgette knew that Angela would call in to see them because it is evident that she was now a proud mum who wanted everyone to meet Johnny.

'Hello Bridgette,' she said.

'I haven't seen you for ages,' replied Bridgette.

'Well, I've been busy'.

I can see that she thought and immediately smiled at the little boy who smiled back.

Johnny had dark hair, large dark brown eyes and a beautiful smile.

'This is Johnny. Johnny, Bridgette's adopted like you,' said Angela.

'Adopted,' mumbled Johnny. He could hardly say the word.

Bridgette was astounded. What did the child learn first? Mummy, Daddy, teddy, then adopted

CHAPTER 8
THE NANNY

A few weeks later, Bridgette was bored. She'd previously enjoyed working at the solicitors, but over the past few weeks, it had become tedious. Many of her friends, who were eighteen and nineteen, were working as nannies in London and she noticed they seemed to be having far more fun than her. Some had already travelled abroad with the families they worked for. This appealed to Bridgette because it would be a chance to break away from home and to explore new places. Although she loved her parents, and her sister Fiona, she wanted to do something more challenging. At nearly eighteen, she needed to prove she could rely on herself and learn new skills.

It was Bridgette's lunch hour, and it was raining. There was very little to do at lunchtime except walk to the corner shop and buy sandwiches for lunch. The small shop also sold hot soup in the winter. It was cold today, and Bridgette wished she'd worn her gloves. The November frost was still lingering on the rooftops and the edges of the pavements. Was she brave enough to tell the solicitors she needed a career change? They would all think she was mad if she told them about being a nanny. She could imagine their reaction, 'why would she want to leave her perfectly good job, as a legal secretary to do that?' Her parents would probably say the same, but it would be exciting, thought Bridgette, and who knows where it might lead, especially if the family went on holidays abroad?

As Bridgette considered her options, she wondered if her parents would be angry. It would be a great opportunity to travel cheaply, plus she'd be getting paid for it! Bridgette hastily picked up a copy of 'The Nanny,' because she had been told by her friends that this magazine frequently had vacancies. It was also a good time of year to apply for positions, when families would be thinking about their summer holidays.

'Two pounds, please,' said the newsagent.

Bridgette was surprised at the cost, but she quickly rolled up the magazine and placed it under her arm, so that she could manage the soup and sandwiches. She had thirty minutes left to sit down and browse through the magazine before it was the end of her lunchbreak. Time went so fast!

Bridgette was a beautiful smart young lady, and she knew it. Men often remarked on her striking looks, and she was often whistled at whilst walking along the road, which she sometimes found embarrassing. The fact that her parents had given her an excellent education, at an all-girls' school, meant she knew how to behave. This was very important to her parents, both being teachers. They had high expectations of her. Some of the girls she went to school with were doing fill-in jobs until they went to university, but Bridgette chose to work as soon as she could because she wanted the money. When she noticed a post for a junior receptionist advertised at the solicitor's office, she jumped at the chance of working there. Now one year later, Bridgette was bored and restless and a nanny job could be just what she needed. One advertisement had already caught her eye:

WANTED NANNY/MOTHERS HELP FOR PROFESSIONAL FAMILY

SURREY/HAMPSHIRE BORDER – LIVE IN

MUST BE YOUNG AND FIT WITH SMART APPEARANCE

GOOD STANDARD OF EDUCATION

SALARY ACCORDING TO AGE AND QUALIFICATIONS

Qualifications thought Bridgette; she had her GCE's, but none in childcare. She didn't have any relevant experience either, apart from a little babysitting for some neighbours on odd occasions. I wonder if that would be enough because I'm keen and I do get on well with small children. Perhaps the fact that I work in a solicitor's office, will stand me in good stead. I am working in a professional environment, and I'm trustworthy.

Bridgette was worried about her parents' reaction. Wages were generally a lot lower than working for a Solicitor, but there wouldn't be living expenses. She would also be closer to her friends in London. They could go to theatres, parties, or dances and have some real fun. Bridgette felt excited about the opportunity. She might even meet a new boyfriend? Her relationship with Mark was near its end. They'd been seeing each other for a year now, and like her job, it was stale. If she got the nanny job, it would give her the opportunity to move on, and hopefully, their relationship would fizzle out.

When she arrived home from work, she decided to tell her mother. If she was seriously applying for jobs, away from home, her Mum had the right to know.

'This isn't a good idea, Bridgette. Have you thought this through? You'd be giving up a job with a better wage. I don't think your dad will be happy, she continued as she started to raise her voice.

'Please don't shout,' replied Bridgette, who was trying to keep control.

'Well, you'd be abandoning a good job, to work for a family, for next to nothing and what will you do after that? Drifting in and out of jobs isn't a good idea.? We paid for that good school for years, which wasn't easy on our wages and now you want to waste your education. Do you really want to be a nanny? It will be hard work, and you'll be working on your own. Where did you say it was again?'

'Surrey,' repeated Bridgette, but she didn't want to discuss it anymore because it was her decision. She didn't expect her parents to understand why she wanted to go, but she also didn't want to back down. Sometimes, you just have to forget about safe and secure, and give things a go, she thought. Her parents had never done that because, because everything they did was planned, nothing was ever spontaneous. But she was different. Bridgette wanted to live her life the way she wanted.

"I'll speak to your father, but I already know what he'll say. He'll think you're irresponsible.'

Bridgette took a long deep breath, then turned on her heels to walk out of the kitchen. She knew there would be a reaction, but not one like this. What was the matter with her? Surely parents wanted their children to be happy?

It was nearly 5.45 pm, and her father was due home in fifteen minutes, when Bridgette put on her long black coat and boots to head towards the front door.

'I'm going for a walk, Mum. Just down the road and back, I won't be long,' she shouted. Her mother mumbled something about dinner being ready soon, but she took no notice. Her purse was full of ten pence pieces, and she went to look for the nearest telephone box. Bridgette decided to phone the number in the advertisement now because there was no point in waiting.

Bridgette walked along their avenue, admiring the houses. They lived in a large detached house, in Ipswich in a good area. Bridgette loved living at home with her parents most of the time. She quickly turned her thoughts to the houses and tried to stop worrying about her father's reaction. She thought their house was the best in the avenue. The exterior pebble dash was painted cream and it had smart new windows, which were still in keeping with a 1930s style house. She had walked this route so many times when she took the bus to work, but she'd never used the phone box. Rebecca knew that her future lay in the ten pence piece she grasped tightly in her hand. She knew her parents would be upset about her leaving, but they'd get over it. After all, it was her life, and she was determined to make the most of it. She began to strive forward positively, thinking of her future and felt a nervous kind of excitement, but she was happy.

    Bridgette glanced at the piece of paper where she'd carefully written Mrs Stephens' number. Her fingers trembled because she was very nervous about calling. She took a few long deep breaths, then dialled the number. There was a pause for a few seconds, then the phone rang at the other end of the line.

    'I'd like to speak to Mrs Stephens please,' she managed to squeak out.

    'Who is it?' asked a voice, which Bridgette assumed was a child.

    'Can you tell her it's Bridgette Woods, I'm calling about the nanny job?'

    The child vanished from the telephone without saying anything. Bridgette could hear crackling in the background and then feet pounding up a set of stairs. After what felt an eternity, there were more footsteps, then the sound of the receiver being lifted.

'Hello, I understand you are interested in the nanny position? First of all, let me explain what I'm looking for. The most important thing is that the person is young, energetic and most of all, reliable. You need to have some experience working with children. Do you have that?" asked Mrs Stephens.

'Yes', I do, replied Bridgette. She listened intently as Mrs. Stephens explained the situation.

'Jonathan's ten and Lucy's eight. They need to be taken to school then collected, every day. There's also Carmel, she's only four, and she's starting school after Easter. She needs to be looked after at home for the next term. She attends a nursery. You'll have the use of a small car. I work in the city and I'll be using the family car. Do you have experience of working with children of this age?' Mrs Stephens inquired, after pausing for breath.

Bridgette thought for a minute. She didn't really know that much about children that age but she had some babysitting experience. She thought it would be more comfortable at this point to say yes, and she added,

'Well, I have cousins of similar age, and I sometimes babysit for them, but I haven't worked as a nanny before.'

'That's fine, as long as you have some experience and you're willing to learn. What have you been doing before?

Bridgette gave Mrs Stephens as much information as she could about her work and also a little about her home life. She seemed keen to listen, and she didn't interrupt her. When she'd finished, she said,

'This job is very different from what you are doing, but as you're the only applicant and I go back to work next week, after the Christmas break, I have got to find someone quickly. I'd like you to come as soon as possible so we can meet. If we get on well with us you can start straight away on a trial basis, for a few weeks. I'll have to see how the children take to you because I want them to be happy. If you do a good job then I'll employ you for the next six months, to begin with. How does that sound?'

Bridgette breathed a sigh of relief. At least she was going to be given a chance, and that's what she wanted. She would work really hard and prove she could be an excellent nanny. It felt like a completely new start, and it felt good.

'Of course, when would you like me to come?' replied Bridgette hoping that she hadn't hesitated too long.

'Come next Tuesday, because the children will be going back to school the following day, around four? I know you are coming a long way, so, between four and five will do just fine.'

Bridgette was relieved that she'd phoned and that Mrs Stephens was so understanding. Her only problem now was her parents!

CHAPTER 9
SISTER MARY - SPRING 1980

Sister Mary lent against her desk. Her back hurt. Years of lifting babies everyday had taken a toll on her health. She used to be able to move around quickly, but now she had pain in her hips, lower back and down one leg. Mary was frequently left in charge because Margaret attended so many meetings. She referred to it as social business. She would still pop in to sign any paperwork and to make sure they were on top of things. In her absence Mary just got on with it, which was more comfortable than seeking lengthy explanations. She woke this morning at 6 a.m. to a bright and sunny day, then she recalled that she'd been placed in charge of St. Catherine's for the foreseeable future. Mary had received a telephone call late last night, to say Margaret was ill, and she wouldn't be coming in for a week or two due to severe bronchitis, so could she take over her duties? She was also asked to call for more help if needed. Mary thought as it was just for a few weeks, they could manage, but beyond that, they would need help because the nuns were already stretched, and it wasn't right to put more pressure on them. With no time to waste, Mary started the usual routine of opening the morning mail before she went to check the babies. The nuns who had more recently joined St. Catherine's, were keen to bottle feed them, at significant expense! St. Catherine's survived mainly by voluntary donations, so their budget was tight. They did their own bit of fundraising by way of jumble sales and garden fetes throughout the year, which helped. All the costings were meticulously calculated by Margaret.

Mary began to look through the post and then sat down in Margaret's usual chair because her leg was hurting. Her memory was terrible, and she frequently forgot the dates of appointments or the whereabouts of pens and pencils. She had no idea why she'd become forgetful. Perhaps she was bored with the routine. This morning, however, something caught her eye. She noticed a letter on the bottom of the pile of post, in a blue envelope with an American stamp. That's strange, she thought, she'd never seen a letter from the States, and what an unusual postage stamp! She tore it off quickly because they saved stamps for charity. After tearing the letter open, she suddenly realised the correspondence was addressed to Margaret, not The Reverend Mother. Mary would generally have put it straight back in the envelope with a scribbled note of apology, but she knew that Margaret wouldn't be returning for a week, possibly longer. The vast majority of letters they received were from young women wishing to trace their parents. They asked if the home still had any their records of their mothers, or a forwarding address. Sometimes the person was so desperate to find out, they persistently telephoned. So, it was agreed that they would only receive mail about adoption inquiries rather than receive telephone calls.

Sister Mary decided to read the letter. She knew that it was an invasion of Margaret's privacy, but she felt driven.

Dear Margaret,

I was so pleased to hear from you last Christmas. I'm delighted that you are continuing your much-needed work at St. Catherine's. Gillian, who as you know has been married for ten years, has decided to adopt her own child and I'll shortly be a grandmother, at last! I often think of that day at the end of the war, when I came to you and begged you for help. I'm so happy that Gillian managed to adopt so quickly because it's a far easier process in Colorado. That is the reason why we decided to move. Gillian only lives two streets away, which is great because I'll be able to see her and my future grandchild regularly, although she plans to work part-time. I couldn't imagine her giving her work up altogether! We are very fortunate that April will be coming to live with Gillian permanently within the next few months. It's so exciting!

I often think that without your help, I would never have her! The thought of being without Gillian is unimaginable! I only hope that she enjoys being a mother because her life will be so different being both a parent and business woman! I know that when the baby arrives, it will be a breath of fresh air to our family after the sadness of Cecil's death. God bless him, he struggled for so many years with cancer. It was a relief for him to be free from that terrible pain.

I know that I've said it many times before, but we'd love you to come and stay with us one day, perhaps when you've finally finished your duties at St. Catherine's! Longmont is fantastic, you'd love it. A break could be just what you need for your health. Gillian is dying to meet you. I frequently tell her that you brought her into this world. What a miraculous story! March 1940 feels like a lifetime ago now. Forty years, would you believe it? Time goes so fast. I must tell you more about our beautiful garden here, which has the most stunning views of the Rocky Mountains...

Mary didn't read the entire letter because she'd read all she could absorb. She saw that Frances, whoever she was, had gone on to write about the plants in her garden, in great detail. The thing which really jumped out at her was the date she mentioned in the letter. March 1940. It was the time she was first admitted to St. Catherine's. She didn't remember much about it now. It was all so long ago and time and her memories were hazy. The death of her baby had been too much for her. The only way she could deal with it was to completely block it from her memory.

There were many discussions about where she could go after the birth of her child, then Margaret took pity on her and said there would be a job for her at St. Catherine's because she found it hard to run the facility, single-handed and Mary gratefully accepted. Her other choice was to return to the convent where her parents sent her, a miserable, dark, cold place in Wiltshire. Some Nuns adapted to the bleak convent, but Mary knew that wasn't the life for her. God had another plan. She preferred to work because it helped her forget and she very quickly looked upon it as her duty to help the girls who were experiencing a similar pain to her own. She was blessed with compassion which she felt was her Christian duty. As the years went on, the pain was still there, but it had become a distant memory.

Mary suddenly clutched the crucifix which hung around her neck, as she experienced the horror of her suppressed feelings. Apart from removing the cross to wash, she never took it off. Mary often prayed that her child was delivered into the kingdom of God and she asked God to give her strength to help the girls. At times, she felt it would be easier to harden her heart towards them and their babies, but her heart remained open. This had been very difficult at times, with each delivery being a reminder of her loss. If only she had held her baby in her arms to say goodbye.

There was a vast amount of work to be done at St. Catherine's and so little time to think. However, today, things felt different. For some unknown reason, her mind was full of curiosity which was unusual. She was struggling today, nothing seemed to make sense. Was she experiencing a loss of faith? She'd heard about other Nuns experiencing this ordeal, but she had never expected it to happen to her. Where did Margaret keep the rest of her private papers? Why couldn't she leave this alone? As her mind chattered away, she became aware that her curiosity was getting the better of her!

It was rare that Mary received a personal letter. At times, she wished people would write, but now with Margaret being ill, she'd excused her actions. She would keep this letter safe and let Margaret have it on her return.

After scurrying around what seemed hours, Mary finally found a small metal key in the top drawer of Margaret's desk. This must be it, she muttered to herself, as she noticed a large wooden box on top of a cupboard where she'd seen Margaret place mail. Mary realised she would have to stand on a little stool to reach it because it was quite a stretch for a short Nun.

The box was gleaming and covered in parquetry; it looked like a mini treasure chest, and it must have dated from the Victorian era. It was beautiful. Mary carefully got down from the stool and placed the box on the desk so that she could safely open it. To her surprise, she saw that there were several letters inside from Frances. She quickly read the dates June 1965, March 1960, December 1955, and some underneath those there was one which appeared to be older, the 12th December 1940. Mary seldom referred to the Reverend Mother as 'Margaret' unless they were alone. Margaret had made it quite clear many years ago, that although they were close, addressing her formally was a matter of respect in front of others. She was very keen that the younger nuns knew their position. Mary was happy to oblige because it was necessary to keep the standards of St. Catherine's high. She had heard of many an establishment where the nuns' behaviour had ruined its reputation. Margaret frequently spoke of these places, and she was determined that St. Catherine's would keep its values.

'I care little for the word 'modern' if it brings disrepute,' she often said. Margaret enjoyed keeping the nuns on their toes. Two other nuns, Sister Emily and Sister Amelia worked at St. Catherine's. They were both younger than Mary, by at least ten years. Mary didn't have the opportunity to chat with them because there was so little time. The two sisters were on loan from another convent this year, and they worked part-time at St. Catherine's. Mary enjoyed their company, even in silence. It reminded her that she was not alone, and it strengthened her service to God to know there were others of a like mind. They felt true companionship in the silences and prayers.

As the years went on, Margaret frequently asked Mary's advice on all sorts them of issues regarding St. Catherine's. Life was never without problems, and many a debate lasted until the early hours of the morning.

Mary sat down and started to read the beginning of a letter from December 1940. She concluded, there was no real harm!

Dear Margaret,

Happy Christmas and a prosperous New Year to you all! I'm writing to let you know that we're all safe and well. I do appreciate the risk you took for us on that windy night in March, and how difficult a decision it was for you. We have decided to call our baby Gillian, she's absolutely beautiful. She's everything that I've ever dreamed of. It would have been impossible, without your help. Cecil dotes on her, he's a marvelous father, and he's been able to establish a good position here, as a banker. I'm sure that he'll rise to the top of his profession, as his father did. I pray that in time, the young nun will make a full recovery from the difficult circumstances and her closeness with God will bring her strength.

Please keep in touch.
God bless,
Frances

Sister Mary clutched her cross and reached for a glass of water. She was definitely having a crisis of faith, but until now she hadn't believed in it.

Following God had always been the most important thing in her life. But now, she saw herself as a twenty-year-old girl, screaming for her baby. There was little memory of that horrific night, apart from the occasional blurred vision. Whatever memory she had of her baby was quickly obscured by a massive white screen where her child vanished. Mary thought that she'd heard her baby's cries and pleaded with the nurse to bring her, but the Reverend Mother quickly appeared at her side with no sign of the baby.

'I'm sorry, but your baby died during the delivery. Unfortunately, there was nothing we could do to save your child. It's in the hands of God now. All we can do is pray.' Mary had no choice but to accept the truth. She was too afraid to ask about the sex of her child because it would have made things harder. She had planned on calling her child William if it was a boy, and she intended to keep him, however difficult. She would return to nursing, where she would earn enough money to make a home for them. It would have been hard, especially on her own, but her baby was part of her and William. Whether she had a boy or girl it didn't matter, she would have done her best so they could remain together, but everything had turned out so differently. She'd lost her baby and had been abandoned by her family, and there was nothing she could do but pray. Mary still remembered the horror of waking up to a very different life. It was very painful.

As Mary read, tears ran down her face. She seldom expressed her feelings because her emotions were so deeply buried. Over the years, they had become a part of her that said 'what a waste of time'. However, when one tear came, there were more, until there was an uncontrollable flood? Could she have been of sound mind, and the cries that she'd heard were from her child? Didn't every mother recognise that sound? This had been proved on numerous occasions at St. Catherine's. Was it also possible that the baby they talked about on that dark, windy March night in 1940, was her baby? What did the letter say again, Mary tried to read it in more detail, but her hands were trembling, and her eyes were losing focus?

'Gillian who launched a cosmetic brand called Super Glow. A successful multinational company. This woman, like her own mother, had to adopt a child. It was ironic, and she couldn't take it in. Gillian was part of a world she knew nothing of. The dates were right though. Was it just a cruel coincidence, a test of faith, or had her child been stolen from her? The idea that Margaret would enter into something like that was inconceivable. At the same time, if she'd discovered the truth, God had forsaken her! She believed her child was dead for the last forty years. Had she been lied to by her oldest friend? The woman she'd looked up to for years. Mary was in a complete state of shock, but what could she do? Perhaps some stones are best left unturned, she concluded as she reached for another hanky.

It was eight-thirty and time to check the babies. They had to be bathed by 10 a.m. She slowly folded the letters and returned them to the box. She then wiped her face. Mary never looked in the mirror because it was considered vain. For now, she wouldn't say anything to Margaret. After all, she couldn't be entirely sure that Gillian was her child, so it would be unfair to mention it with her being so ill. Margaret might also ask why was she was reading her letters! Frances could have been talking about someone entirely different, but she doubted it. Even if it were true, what life had she known apart from St. Catherine's? Within minutes she'd fallen back into her usual routine. Her hands were washed and she closed the door. It was too late to think about those things now, when there was so much work to do, she concluded as she quickly straightened her habit.

CHAPTER 10
GILLIAN – 1980

Gillian looked with pride at her new nursery. Everything was perfect for April. Unfortunately, she suffered similar fertility problems as her mother, which was a strange and cruel coincidence. She was now forty years of age, and most of her friends had children in their twenties. Gillian and her husband, Ron, had tried to have children for many years, without success. She was told that once she got over the age of thirty, the chances of her conceiving were slim. After much heartache, Gillian and Ron decided to add their names to the adoption list. They'd been on the list for a year, when they heard some news about the possibility of adopting a baby girl.

Ron had his own car hire business in Colorado, which was very successful. He rented out limousines for weddings, parties and events. Gillian was also a great businesswoman, who owned a large multinational company called Super Glow, that had quickly spread from the States into Europe. Super Glow had recently been ranked number one, by a major consumer magazine, whose ratings were followed internationally. This was exciting for her because her sales would rise. It was proving to be an exceptional year. The more publicity Super Glow received, the better. Her dream was to change the way women felt about beauty, especially English women who were way behind the States and she planned to bridge the gap. When it came to cosmetics, Gillian led the field in adventurous products. Many women, particularly in the UK, didn't wear much make-up. They didn't want to spend money on eyelashes, or nails, so Gillian decided to launch her skin and hair products until the British market caught up. Surely, in the eighties with so much choice in fashion, these women needed the right cosmetics. No-one wanted to be stuck in a time warp when what they craved was glamour!

Gillian slowly ran her hand over the white cot that stood in the corner of the well-prepared nursery. It had cost a fortune, but it was worth it. The finish felt smooth to the touch, as smooth as little April. What a beautiful name. Hopefully, she wouldn't have to wait much longer because the continual not knowing was killing her. Mother was right about the baby; she would be like a breath of fresh air. I wonder how she will handle being adopted, thought Gillian suddenly. She reflected on her own story, as she tried to remember the details.

Gillian knew about her adoption from a young age. Her mother was a young girl who gave birth to her then tragically died from complications. Gillian had always thought it was an extremely sad story, but at least she knew the truth, which made it easier to understand. She wasn't a person who generally expressed her emotions, but it brought tears to her eyes. For the last twenty years of her life, since she'd left University, she had a strong desire to achieve something worthwhile that would not only help others, but would live on after her. Gillian never stopped working. She was dedicated to her business. If they hadn't adopted April, she would have looked for new opportunities to expand. Gillian was well aware of her success which gave her a strong feeling of security. This was something she also wanted for her child. In the last few years, she'd become aware of her biological clock ticking. At the age of forty she had already decided that if it didn't happen by forty-five, she would abandon the idea of being a parent and start an entirely new business venture. She found it hard to understand why pregnancy was difficult when other things in her life had been achievable. Had putting her career first become a distraction from the truth? She now desperately wanted a child.

Her mother often talked about the benefits of adopting. At first, she didn't want to even consider it. Although her mother Frances was well-grounded and gave excellent advice, Gillian was unsure, until she discovered the problems with her ovaries and it became her only option. At last, she had to admit defeat or another few years would slip by.

'Gillian, look at it this way, you can keep trying month after month, but at the end of the day you're wasting valuable time. There's a child out there who needs two loving parents and the longer you wait, the more frustrated you'll become. Believe you me I know because I went through the same thing. It wasn't a natural choice for me either, but you came from such tragic circumstances. When Margaret contacted me to say there was a baby girl who was perfect for us, I had to make a quick decision. As you know, there isn't a day that goes by when I don't think about what a wonderful daughter you are. Now, it's your turn to be a mother, and you're not getting any younger. Being an older mother is hard work, adopt now, while you're still can!' Frances said encouragingly. The heaviness in Gillian's heart was unbearable. Her mother did make sense, and every option had been explored. Now, after all the waiting was over, April was finally coming. They had decided to call the baby April because this was the month that she was due to arrive on trial adoption. It was only a few weeks away, and Gillian was counting the days. They would have the baby for six weeks to start. If they bonded well as a family and the natural mother agreed, it would go to court for the final adoption order to be made. They would then be April's official parents. Gillian was both excited and apprehensive. Surely all new parents felt like this? After all, she was a first-timer, and although April felt like a promise, there was still uncertainty. What if the mother changed her mind? It didn't bear thinking about!

Gillian wanted to give her daughter the best of everything. The nursery was finally complete after many months of decorating and visiting a whole string of top department stores. Although she knew that April would be showered with many gifts, Gillian had learned that the most important gift a mother could give to her child was confidence. She needed to know she'd succeed. April will never feel insecure, lost or lonely, because we are two now. We'll understand each other and have an exceptional bond. Two adopted children bound by circumstance and overwhelming love!

CHAPTER 11
REBECCA & LAWRENCE

Rebecca clicked the clasp of her gold bracelet tightly. It was a special gift from Lawrence. She'd never married, but over the years, Rebecca had been involved in several relationships. There had been a few more recently, but she'd never met anyone she loved until she met Lawrence. He was different being both attractive and mature, and he loved her. He wasn't only her boyfriend, but her best friend. Despite this, there were still some areas of her life that she found it painful to share. When they first met, Rebecca was working as an assistant manager in one of the big banks, in the centre of London. Rebecca had worked extremely hard over the years, and she now had a well-paid and enjoyable job. She was dedicated to her career and expected to make the position of Branch Manager within the next year. Rebecca seldom looked back. Her life was full and busy. She had many friends and had recently joined a local social club where a group of them attended dances, dinners and theatre trips.

Rebecca rarely thought about her work at the factory. She'd learned so much about life while living on her own, and there was always plenty to do. She was no longer the naive, young woman who worked for low wages with little knowledge of men. It was hard to imagine that the foolish girl existed and she'd convinced herself that she hadn't. The girl who got carried away by her dreams and fantasies had long gone. Imagine thinking that Michael would provide for her! It sounded like madness. How would her life have been better with him? At times, her former childlike naivety made her laugh. Michael, her employer, would have left his wife for her. It was a joke!

Almost twenty years on and Rebecca's life had taken so many different turns, which was partly due to Lawrence. Lawrence was now a successful actor who'd managed to obtain some roles on television shows. His success was partly due to his amazing voice. After his early years in radio, he'd progressed to advertisements, and more recently documentaries. His talents were in demand.

It all started when he began mimicking famous people at the university. He constantly made the other students laugh! He was fortunate enough to have been brought up in a middle-class family who encouraged his education. He was a bright talented boy, who was later went to Oxford. While studying there, he joined a local amateur dramatic group. One day, during a drama session, a visitor who worked for local radio, attended and noticed Lawrence's talent.

Lawrence was giving one of his better performances but he never took himself that seriously and when Lawrence was suddenly offered a job, he was astounded. At first, he worked for a local radio station in Oxford and later on Radio 4, reading stories on Sunday afternoons. A few years later he started working for the BBC. He'd had some lucky breaks, and was grateful. His soft tone could easily captivate an audience. Rebecca also loved his voice, which also sounded romantic and comforting.

Lawrence's mother was Irish. Rebecca wondered if his charming tone were due to his slight Irish accent, that she was so familiar with. This man enchanted and excited her. He was fit, lean and artistic by nature loved landscape painting. His dream was to retire to Scotland, to paint the outstanding scenery. He also loved salmon fishing, but what Rebecca admired most about him, was his sheer enthusiasm for life. She'd never met anyone quite like him. He had boundless energy. He admired her too, and treated her with respect. He never forgot about the essential things. He telephoned her regularly, and was rarely late. He also bought her beautiful gifts that were imaginatively and sensitively selected. In many ways, Lawrence was the perfect partner. She felt loved.

Rebecca was aware that her childbearing years were passing, and Lawrence didn't have any children, nor did he want any. She thought that there was now little chance of her conceiving any further children, and this was a relief to her. They were happy as they were, and their lives were full. Rebecca decided to let the children issue go. They didn't live together because she still had her own flat in East London, but was happy to see Lawrence at the weekends. Rebecca would also stay the weekend at his apartment in North London.

Rebecca often thought of the day he'd first walked into the bank. Lawrence had breezed in confidently then said, 'Rebecca, you're a stunning woman. Please will you accompany me to the theatre tonight. I have two tickets?' Rebecca wasn't at all offended by his brash request because he was a regular, and they'd always chatted. Secretly, she was very attracted to him, but she'd been careful not to reveal it. The pain of what had happened in 1962, had taught her some valuable lessons about men. One of them was not to be too idealistic, things were seldom as they seemed, and to keep her independence at any cost! However, she was tempted by this charming man who always smelt of good aftershave and wore finely tailored clothes. So, an exception had to be made. Rebecca agreed to go to the theatre with Lawrence. She was so enthralled by the experience; she couldn't wait to see him again.

As the weeks turned into months, their occasional date quickly changed into something more serious, but never once did she tell Lawrence the story of Bridgette, the baby she'd lost. The baby, she pretended was dead. If she opened up to him, it would drive a wedge between them. Although she loved Lawrence, her past was not relevant to her future. A future she hoped they'd spend together. She'd already been through enough pain, without destroying what they'd built.

As the years went by, it was only really on Bridgette's birthday that Rebecca thought about her. This year was particularly hard because she knew that Bridgette would be eight and considered an adult. It was unbelievable to think that she'd be able to make her own decisions, have the key to the house or even leave home and get her own place. It didn't seem possible. Most alarming of all was the fact that Bridgette could now legally trace her, which would destroy her life? It was too confusing to think about. Her vision of Bridgette was the small baby that she'd held so tightly in those last few hours, and she wanted to keep it that way.

CHAPTER 12
THE JOURNEY

It was raining heavily, and not the best day in the world to attend an interview that was miles away, thought Bridgette as she stepped onto the train to travel to London Liverpool Street. Water had splashed up her tights, and her shoes were soaked inside and out, which felt horrible. It would have been a better idea to wear boots, she thought, as she took off her wet gloves to lay them on the seat beside her. She hoped they'd be dry by the time they reached London.

The journey was around ninety minutes so she sat back and tried to relax. Bridgette had already decided she wanted this job. She was ready to take anything to get away from home and start an independent life. Her mother and father were still annoyed at her for giving up her secretarial job, to work as a nanny, but they had softened a little.

'It isn't a good move, Bridgette. Childcare is such low paid work, and it won't get you anywhere.' her mother repeated.

Bridgette pondered. Where was she trying to get? At least by doing this, she'd have the experience. That was what life was about, wasn't it, having experiences? She wanted an adventure to break up the long boring routine that everyone called work! She knew she was taking a chance, which was scary, but it had to be taken.

The train pulled up at many familiar stations along the route. Having travelled to London with her parents, on several occasions, Bridgette recognised the stations. Manningtree was the first one with lovely views over the Stour. The station was pretty too. Next was Colchester, then Chelmsford, they were getting closer to London now. When she finally arrived at Liverpool Street, she had to take the tube to the outskirts of London, where she'd eventually take a taxi to her destination. What a performance!

Bridgette was a little apprehensive about starting the nanny job straight away. What if Mrs Stephens didn't like her, then she could be on the next train home? Bridgette didn't want this to happen because she'd finished her job at the Solicitors so there was no choice but to make a go of it!

After what felt like hours later, Bridgette walked up the path of a gorgeous house and was pleasantly surprised by what she saw. The house was well set back from the road in a quiet cul-de-sac. The homes were relatively modern, likely built within the last twenty years. It was a large detached house built in a traditional style which resembled a country cottage. The front garden was tiny and completely open without hedges or walls, but to the rear she could see it had a long garden which was enclosed by a high brick wall. The sound of screams and laughter came from behind the wall as she rang the doorbell.

Mrs Stephens opened the door widely and stood facing her. She was an attractive woman in her late thirties with a generous amount of dyed blonde hair piled on her head. It gave her an air of sophistication. Her make-up was immaculate, and she wore a silver necklace with matching earrings which highlighted her beautiful tanned skin.

'Bridgette?'

Bridgette drew in a long breath. Her stomach had been churning for hours. Her logical mind told her it was butterflies, but the pain had turned into a crippling stomach ache. Her throat was also dry, which made it difficult to speak. Instead of a strong yes, her reply was more like a whimper.

'Yes, I'm pleased to meet you,' she said, holding out her hand.'

'The children are in the garden. We'll go and have a chat first, then I'll introduce you. They can't be out there for long because it's so cold,' she said, giving Bridgette a warm smile.

Bridgette was taken into a square hallway, with fitted carpets and rugs. The stairs were open plan with spaces between. The choice of paintings on the walls was fascinating. The pictures were of seascapes painted in oil, and they were all similar. Their bold colours brightened what would otherwise have been a plain area. Mrs Stephens politely took Bridgette's coat and then proceeded to lead her into a living room which overlooked the garden. There was a sizeable comfortable cream sofa and chairs. Everything in the lounge was simple in design, but some effort had been made to brighten the space with more paintings and dried grasses. There were also some painted beams on the high ceiling which had been artexed. Apart from the room being of no particular era, Bridgette felt it was warm and comfortable, with its beiges and browns.

The patio doors opened onto a large garden which was mainly laid to lawn with a garden shed at the end. This was approached by a colourful brick path which made Bridgette think of the yellow brick road, from the Wizard of Oz. What fun for the children! Could this house be her Oz? She knew a new challenge awaited her, which would be a totally new experience. Looking after three children would be hard work, but it could also be fun. She'd play lots of games with them and hopefully they'd grow to like her.

'Do take a seat,' asked Mrs Stephens, bringing Bridgette down to earth!

Bridgette chose one of the cream chairs and sank down into it. She immediately lost some of her height, while Mrs Stephens, perched on the edge of her chair, giving Bridgette the impression that she found it hard to relax. Bridgette admired her long legs which were covered in black stockings. She also wore a short black skirt and a casual cardigan, giving her an air of respectability.   'First of all, please call me Karen because no-one in this house calls me Mrs

Stephens and I'd like you to be relaxed when you are with us. Please make our home yours during your time here. I've made a schedule to show you when to take the children to school and a map of how to get there. Neil will take you the first time until you find your bearings. There is a car you can use for school trips. The old Fiesta in our second garage. It used to be mine a few years ago, but it's now kept for nannies. You'll have the use of this car whenever you need it, and we'll keep it topped up with petrol. Look upon it as an extra, on top of your wages. You can also use it at the weekends if you want to go to London or the coast, although going into the city is easier by train. It's insured for any driver, so there is no problem with you using it from the word, go,' explained Karen enthusiastically.

Bridgette was suddenly pleased that her parents made her take driving lessons. Although she hadn't driven much in Suffolk when she worked for the solicitors. Mark owned a car, so there wasn't the necessity. She was a little out of practice, but she would pick it up again. Wow, what freedom! She liked the sound of a job where would she could go anywhere and everywhere, even into the city!

'The next thing is, I appreciate your time will be your own at the weekends but I do expect you to work hard during the week. You'll have to learn to put the children first. Jonathan and Lucy get on very well, but they do have arguments. When you bring them home from school, you will have to...'

Bridgette listened with interest to what Karen had to say. She suddenly realised that being a nanny entailed an awful lot more than she had envisaged, but she'd give it her best.

'Now let me tell you about Carmel, she's a little hyperactive, which can be a problem, but it's fine as long as she gets your attention. If not, she can be a little stubborn. I think it's because she feels different from the others. Jonathon and Lucy are from my first marriage, but Carmel is Neil's daughter. Oh yes, and Neil is younger than me, that's why he's energetic. He's always at the gym. Neil often works at home, but he's swamped, hence why we need a nanny. The other nanny left because she was pregnant. She'd been with us for a couple of years and she loved the job. I hope you'll like it too,' Karen explained, in a gentle voice.

'I'm sure I will,' Bridgette replied, not knowing what to say. She hoped to like it, but everything sounded much harder work than she anticipated. At least weekends would be free and would have the use of a car. She thought about Carmel. It must be hard for her feeling different from her brother and sister, but it wasn't the same as being adopted. Being adopted meant you always felt different. Still, Bridgette's heart went out to the girl because she could empathise. Mrs Stephens began to talk as if she was starting straight away. Bridgette hoped this was the case. She'd sent her some brilliant references, which must have helped.

Karen already knew that Bridgette would make a good Nanny. She was the right age and had worked in a respectable job. Her experience of children was a little limited, but the girl was obviously intelligent and willing. She had no doubt that Bridgette would quickly pick things up. More importantly, she came from a good background, and that would work well with them because she didn't want the children to pick up any bad habits. Bridgette appeared mature, and she communicated well, so she was prepared to give her a trial.

'Can I meet the children now?' asked Bridgette after a very long silence.

'Yes, of course, you can, I told them that you are coming and they are excited about meeting you,' Karen replied.

Bridgette suddenly felt like a woman on a mission; as if everything was meant to be. She would phone her parents tonight and tell them the news to reassure them there was nothing to worry about. She felt sure that in time they'd come around to the idea.

The children were all playing together in the garden. Surprisingly, they hardly noticed their mother or Bridgette! Jonathan was on a bike riding around in circles, Lucy was on roller-skates singing to herself while skating up and down the colourful path, and Carmel was bouncing a ball on the patio.

'What are you doing, Carmel?' asked Bridgette, who was immediately drawn to the little girl.

'I'm playing basketball.'

'Oh, are you, are you good at catch?'

'Sometimes,' answered Carmel shyly, as she put down the ball and watched it roll into the flowerbed.

'My name's Carmel. I'm four. I'm going to a big school soon.'

Great thought Bridgette, at least she's talking to me. This feels like a good start. Then suddenly she heard a loud voice coming from the other side of the patio doors. Bridgette immediately noticed, there was a man with black shorts and muscular legs and Neil stepped into the garden.

'Karen, where are you? We need to get a shift on if we're going out later', he said.

'Oh, it's Neil. He's home early! I remember now, we're going out! Do come and meet him, Bridgette because I'm sure you two will get on well,'' said Karen enthusiastically, as they stepped back into the house.

'Neil, this is our new nanny, Bridgette. She's come all the way from Suffolk so that she can start with us straight away. Can you show her how to get into the garage please, and let her have a key to the Fiesta? I've got to pop up and finish cleaning her room, nearly done. Bridgette was here in good time, in fact, a bit earlier than I expected. I've just got to change the bed,' explained Karen, smiling at them both.

Neil turned to face Bridgette. He was still in his gym gear, a pair of shorts, sports socks, fashionable trainers and a black vest top. His arms were also muscular, and he looked fit. His scooped vest revealed a slightly hairy chest and his blonde hair was fashionably gelled back, which made him look young, possibly in his late twenties. Two strong eyebrows framed a pair of intelligent blue eyes. Neil had a serious, but artistic look about him. He also had a deep frown which gave Bridgette the impression that he worried a lot. He suddenly looked towards her and smiled as if to read her thoughts. When he smiled his whole face lit up and his frown disappeared. As he looked into her eyes, Bridgette felt almost disorientated, and for a few moments, she forgot where she was. As Neil was her new employer, she was slightly embarrassed by the length of her gaze, and she quickly glanced down to change the dynamic of their encounter.

'I hope you won't get bored here, Bridgette. I'll give you a list of places to go at the weekends if you like? What do you like doing? Movies, theatre, or perhaps walks in the countryside? There are some great places to see around here. I generally work from home. I have an office upstairs but I can't have the kids bothering me while I'm working. Carmel needs loads of attention; I expect Karen has explained about that?'

Bridgette was beginning to wonder what on earth she had let herself in for, when Karen suddenly appeared and said, 'I don't need you to do anything for us now until we go out at seven o'clock, so I'll show you to your room. You can eat with us tonight, then we'll leave it up to you, as long as you feed the children at the times on the schedule. You may want to eat out sometimes. I'm sure you'll soon make friends.

Bridgette noticed her room had twin beds, an ensuite shower and toilet. It looked spotless with blue and white flowered Laura Ashley wallpaper. The bed was covered with a blue bedspread, and it had a beige carpet. There was also a large built-in wardrobe with mirrors and a small, old looking portable television which stood on top of a chest of drawers.

'I hope you'll be comfortable here. If you need anything, please let me know, I'm only in the kitchen.'

'I think I'll be fine,' replied Bridgette, who looked very happy with her surroundings. This is far better than my room at home, she thought. She'd never experienced the luxury of an adjoining bathroom. Things were looking up!

Bridgette's thoughts turned to Mark. She'd found it difficult to say goodbye, but she knew it was for the best because the relationship had become stale. It felt more like brother and sister, than girlfriend and boyfriend so she'd hoped it would fizzle out. He promised to write, and if he did, she wouldn't reply. It felt mean, but he needed to move on.

Bridgette lay on the bed and wondered if she was going to be a good nanny. She wanted to make this job work, and her parents proud of her. Fitting in had always been a challenge. She wondered why this was, yet on some level she already knew. It was something that never went away and because of that, she never felt good enough. Bridgette sighed and lay down on the bed. She'd a couple of hours now in which to have a short sleep. Mark had become a fading memory as her thoughts turned to Neil!

CHAPTER 13
SEVERAL WEEKS LATER

'Good morning, Bridgette,' shouted a loud male voice which came right through her bedroom door! 'What a beautiful morning. It's sunny, and we don't often see the sun this time of year. The children are up and dressed already so we'll see you at breakfast shortly.'

Bridgette couldn't believe how cheerful Neil was. He always appeared to be happy first thing in the morning which amazed her because her parents were seldom lively at this time of day! Bridgette wiped the sleep from her eyes, took a quick shower and quickly got dressed. Over the past few weeks, she'd begun to form a good relationship with the children and she had started to relax.

The school run took place at eight-thirty, so she had to be up by seven to make sure the children were dressed and had eaten their breakfast. The Fiesta was a godsend. Bridgette loved driving and it was usually fun taking the children to school, unless they argued! Jonathan sat in the front, and Lucy and Carmel who was strapped in a child's seat, sat in the back. Jonathan loved to talk, he noticed new things, every day. Birds, trees, the names of roads, or anything slightly different. Bridgette was amazed at the things he knew about wildlife, but she had recently discovered that Neil also loved bird watching, and the family were members of the RSPB. Jonathan told her that Neil was an artist, and he frequently spent time by the sea, painting. They were his seascapes in their hall. They certainly were an active family with non-stop activities, school plays, theatre clubs, social and church events, the list went on and on. Although Bridgette wasn't expected to attend that many of them, she still had to plan her life around their activities. They were nearly at the school now, and Carmel was arguing with her sister, 'Give it back, or I'll hit you,' she shouted in her baby voice.

'I'm scared,' replied Lucy. This went on most mornings, and sometimes Jonathan would join in, or he'd turn around and tell them to shut up, which made it hard for her to concentrate on driving. Carmel usually burst into tears, until she couldn't hear anything else but her wailing! That child needs to go to school, she muttered. But she knew that when she'd dropped off the older two and returned home with Carmel, she'd read her stories. They'd make playdough together, or do a giant jigsaw and Carmel would become calm and attentive. Then very quickly it would be twelve o'clock, and it was time to prepare lunch.

Life was full, but Bridgette loved it. It was so different from her previous job. What she did miss, though, were her friends. She'd heard her friends were going out in the evenings to discos and clubs and having tremendous fun and she was stuck on her own. They used to go by train to Felixstowe, a local seaside town, and they always had such fun together. Then, there were boys! Was she ever going to meet someone here, stuck out in the sticks? The Fiesta called to her saying I'm here, take me out. Where do you want to go? How about this weekend, jump in! But Bridgette was afraid of going out on her own. She was all right with the school runs, but driving further was challenging. Perhaps in the summer, she'd go down to the south coast, Hastings, or somewhere nearby.

For the past few weeks, Bridgette had spent most of her weekends going into the local town, which was small and not exactly bustling with life but it was still better than spending her spare time in her room. She'd spent some of her earnings on clothes and shoes and then she reminded herself that she wanted to save! It was hard.

Bridgette cleared away the children's finished plates, which were now empty of fish fingers, chips and beans. The children were happily playing with the toys in the lounge when Neil returned from work. She didn't often see him in his work clothes because he usually went to the gym on his way home and shot straight upstairs for a shower. Today, he walked into the house wearing a neat pinstriped business suit, cuff links, and a plain navy tie with a silver tie pin. She'd never seen one of these before because her father never wore things like that, preferring to dress plainly.

'Hello, young lady. I see you haven't clocked up many miles on the old Fiesta yet.' said Neil as he entered the kitchen.

Bridgette felt a little-observed, but she smiled at Neil.

'I'll tell you what; Karen will be at a conference this weekend, and my mother is coming to stay to look after the children. So, if you're up for it, on Sunday, I'll take you out for a spin in the MG. We'll go for a walk or something? I could show you the local area and have a pub lunch? How does that sound?'

Bridgette thought hard. She wanted to say yes, but then it occurred to her that Karen may consider it inappropriate behaviour for a nanny and she didn't want to shirk her responsibilities.

'I'm not sure, Neil. Do you think Karen will mind me not staying at home with the children?'

'No, not at all, in fact, it was her idea that I took you out! She thought you looked a bit peaky lately and could do with some fresh air. The March winds will certainly blow the cobwebs away.' replied Neil, smiling.

So, Bridgette agreed to go out on Sunday and secretly she felt very excited about it. Was it because she'd become attracted to him, she wondered? Or, was it that her only trips out were to take the children to school or birthday parties? Whatever the reason was for this feeling, she couldn't wait to go!

Sunday came around very quickly. Although rain was forecast, it appeared to be a warm day and the sun was out. Bridgette realised it wouldn't be long until she returned home to see her family because it was nearing the end of her trial period. Although, if they kept her on, she might as well stay until Easter, because she was settled in her new job. Her mother was pleased that she phoned her regularly and brought her up to date. Bridgette missed her family and friends, but she'd bonded with the children and Karen and Neil were always helpful. Plus, Carmel was settling down at last, and they often watched television programs together, which Bridgette enjoyed. It made her feel like a child again! The job was excellent, but she hadn't realised how much she'd miss home.

It was Sunday, and Neil's dark green opened top MG stood in the driveway. Bridgette could see him giving it the once over before they went out. He adjusted the mirrors, looked for patches of rust then cleared the windscreen. There were no visible signs of corrosion, because he kept his car in pristine condition. Every week it was washed and polished from top to bottom. His MG was his pride and joy.

Bridgette wondered about Karen and Neil's relationship. They never seemed to be in the house at the same time! She knew they occasionally went out as a couple to social events because she was paid a little extra to babysit, but it was rare. She never saw them watch television, or shared stories about the children, or have the togetherness her own parents had. Bridgette concluded that they held each other at a distance, for what reason she was unsure.

Neil beeped his horn to signal he was ready to leave. Bridgette quickly slipped on a short black jacket with a fur collar, that she'd bought the previous week and rushed towards the car. She was dressed for a country walk in corduroy trousers, a polo neck jumper and boots! She quickly jumped in because Neil was revving the engine. If he was going to keep the roof down, it might be cold but the sun was warm today despite being early in the year.

'I thought you'd changed your mind,' said Neil, jokingly. Bridgette wasn't very good with jokes because she was young and sensitive, so she frowned and didn't reply. She looked at Neil who was wearing, a tan leather jacket, a polar neck jumper, well-fitting jeans and tan shoes which coordinated with his jacket and she felt very attracted to him.

'I thought it might be chilly,' he said, doing up his zip.

'Where are we going?' asked Bridgette, enthusiastically.

'You'll see. I'm taking you on a mystery tour! Don't look so worried, Bridgette, you'll love it.' he said, trying to put her at ease.

They drove through country lanes for the best part of an hour, admiring hedgerows and wildflowers. There were snowdrops on grassy banks and spring flowers were everywhere. Suddenly, she could see an entrance to a small car park amongst the trees.

'Are we stopping here?' she asked.

'Yes, we're going squirrel hunting, then later we'll go and get something to eat, fancy that? It will be fun!' said Neil.

'Of course, I've brought my old boots in case it gets muddy,' replied Bridgette.

'Clever girl,' he replied giving her a slight nudge.

Bridgette looked at Neil. He was grinning like a Cheshire cat. She would have to watch that, she thought as a strange feeling arose inside her. This was something new to Bridgette. It felt out of control, and she started to tingle with excitement.

Mark had written to her once since she'd been staying with the family, but she hadn't bothered to reply. His news was always boring. Being with Neil was new and exciting. She knew it was wrong to have feelings for him because he was married, but she couldn't help it.

When she first met Mark, he meant everything to her. There was definitely something lovely about him. Her friends said he was the boy-next-door type, and they were right. They'd go for a drink at the local pub, or to his house to watch television, but they never did anything interesting. They were meant to save for a holiday in Greece, next year, but she knew that Mark wouldn't save a penny because he was hopeless with money. She didn't understand what he did with it but he never had any. Perhaps it was running a car or something, she wasn't sure, but it was frustrating.

Bridgett began tussling her hair and straightening her back because she wanted Neil to notice her. She felt happy when she was around him and she wanted physical contact. But why would Neil be interested in her, after all, he was married, and she was his seventeen-year-old Nanny! He was also her employer. What was she thinking of? She suddenly came down to earth with a jolt when he spoke to her.

'Ready then?' he repeated a little louder, as he sensed Bridgette was miles away.

Bridgette pulled on her one size too small rubber boots. She knew she would be in pain after walking a few miles, but there was no choice because purchasing new boots hadn't been her priority when there were clothes, handbags and make-up to buy! She'd also forgotten the last time she'd actually worn them, probably on some boring walk, with her parents.

Neil started to walk along a windy path which led into a wood. The wood was full of enormous pine trees. It was beautiful. There were a lot of sticks and twigs under their feet which had blown off in the winds. There was also fresh new growth, peeping through at the edges of the wood and Bridgette saw some wild rabbits hopping in the distance. They're probably looking for a mate, she thought, it's spring!

'Look up to the sky. Up there, amongst the treetops. There's one,' shouted Neil.

Bridgette looked up into the pine trees. They were extraordinarily tall, and they seemed to go on forever. It was very hard, even with her neck craned, to see their tops but scampering up about halfway from the top, was their first grey squirrel.

'Yes, I can see him now. Are there a lot of squirrels here?'

'There are absolutely loads of them. That's why I brought you here so that you can count them. At the end of the walk, we'll see who has counted the most! If you see a red one, they are so rare, that can count as two!' said Neil laughing.

'Okay, but I warn you, I'm good at squirrel counting,' replied Bridgette, brightening up as they began to laugh together. Their voices could be heard echoing around the wood as Bridgette tried to catch her breath.

'That smell, it makes you think of...'

'Warm baths,' said Neil, as he darted away quickly to take up a slow jog.

'I bet you can't catch me, young lady,' he added as his voice trailed off.

'That's not fair, I have a stitch, and my boots are too tight,' said Bridgette, who was trying her best to keep up with him. Bridgette realised how unfit she was and suddenly felt ashamed. There had been no time to exercise since she became a nanny. because Her life revolved around making meals, trips to school, clubs and other activities and she felt too tired to join a gym or go swimming.

'Slow down,' shouted Bridgette

'What's the matter with you? I thought young people were meant to be fit!' said Neil, who was now about ten metres in front of her.

'Not this one,' she replied hastily.

She then found a sudden spurt of energy and raced to catch him up.

'There you see. You've been running you missed a squirrel!' Bridgette shouted, in an effort to slow him down!

'That's the trouble, you're right. I do miss things,' replied Neil with a sad tone to his voice as he fell in step with her.

'I'm sorry,' replied Bridgette, but she didn't ask what Neil missed because she was aware not only of the age gap between them but her status as a nanny. For a few minutes, there was silence, and then Neil turned around to look into her eyes.

'Do you really like this sort of thing, Bridgette?' he asked.

'I love it,' she replied, smiling at him. She most certainly did! Bridgette hadn't felt this happy, not for a long time. She wished their walk would last forever. She listened to him explain the many types of trees, animal habitats and cloud formations. The clouds looked like cotton wool today, a place where dreams were made. Is it possible to catch a cloud, thought Bridgette? Eventually, it would disperse like a bubble because nothing lasts forever. Please make it stay long enough for me to be happy, she thought whimsically. Her mother had always called her a daydreamer when she looked up at the clouds. Perhaps she was.

Neil turned towards her as if to read her thoughts.

'What are your thoughts about soul mates, Bridgette? Do you think they exist?'

Bridgette was taken aback by his profound question.

'Yes, but I think we have more than one, don't you?' she replied thoughtfully.

'Interesting answer and very mature. Shall we hurry back to the car now. I think it's starting to rain? I don't like the look of that black cloud over there. Are you ready for the pub?'

Bridgette nodded her head to say yes, because she was out of puff. When she focused on the sound of Neil's voice. It sounded familiar and melodious like a song.

'I'm happy to go with the flow,' she said.

'That's what I like about you Bridgette,' Neil whispered, as he leaned towards her, then quickly pulled away again. Bridgette could hear her heart pounding in her chest. He does like me, she thought and wondered why he didn't kiss her. Did she like him, or had her feelings reached a completely new level!

They searched for a pub and Neil found one a few miles away that he'd visited before. It took no time at all to get there, and it was already full of people eating Sunday lunch. It was hard to find a free table that didn't have 'reserved' on it. One end of the pub was taken up with a roaring fire set in a huge inglenook fireplace. Horse brasses hung around the public house which, according to Neil, used to be an old coach house. The landlord was friendly enough and seemed to know him from his previous visits.

'Good day, how are things with you?' he asked in a friendly voice. They exchanged pleasantries, then Neil showed Bridgette to a table in the corner of the room, where the Landlord pointed for them to sit.

Neil talked to Bridgette about the area. The best places to eat, some good walks and local history. She was fascinated by this man. He was confident and able to talk to her on her level. He also appeared caring as he listened to her answers with interest. This made Bridgette feel older than her years, and once again she reflected on what a lucky woman Karen was!

'We think you're doing a great job with the children, especially Carmel, whose noticeably improved since you've been with us. She seems a lot calmer now. Plus, she doesn't argue with the other two like she used to,' said Neil.

Bridgette immediately felt flattered. She knew this was true because the children were beginning to respond to Carmel positively, although she found it tiring and longed for a bit of time on her own. She was grateful that Neil was showing her these places because she could return to them if she had a free weekend.

'It's difficult because Karen suffers from terrible migraines, so she doesn't have much patience with the children. She also works too hard, and we don't spend enough time together as a family.' Neil continued.

Bridgette noticed the frown had returned. Part of her wanted to comfort him. Although he didn't say so, she felt that he was a little lonely. He was obviously finding it difficult to communicate with Karen. She wanted to touch his hand, but she didn't want him to take it the wrong way.

An hour later, they finished their lunch and headed home. The wind blew directly into their faces. The MG took a few of the bends a bit sharply, which scared her but it was exhilarating! Wow, thought Bridgette, I'm freezing but for the first time in ages, I feel alive. Her heart was racing. Bridgette watched Neil's leather gloves on the steering wheel. He's so good looking, she thought, wishing that he'd kissed her!

CHAPTER 14
THE SUMMER

It was a long summer. Bridgette had enjoyed taking the children out on outings and being part of a new family. Over the past few weeks, things had fallen into a routine which worked well for them all. She decided to return home for a few weeks because Neil and Karen were taking some time off work so they didn't need her.

Bridgette missed her family and friends. Going home would give her the chance to catch up with their news. It was ages since she'd seen her friends. She'd considered popping to see Mark, but as their relationships had fizzled, she was unsure how he'd react! It would be hard to avoid him when they had the same friends. Perhaps it was better to meet with him and chat than to face embarrassment. There was no reason why they couldn't remain friends. A girlfriend recently told her that Mark was getting on very well with his career and he'd been promised promotion. He needed some good luck to come his way because he'd always been short of money.

Bridgette knew it would be a wrench to be away from Neil, even for a few weeks, because her attraction to him had grown stronger. She knew she was playing with fire, but she couldn't help her feelings. The age gap between them plus his marital status told her he was a definite no, but Bridgette chose to think Neil was unhappily married. It was evident that he and Karen had little in common. She needed to get over him. It was stupid and dangerous to have these feelings and she wanted to do the right thing. Perhaps going home would help her get over him, she hoped so! She really missed her sister. Fiona had taken some time off work so they could do the girly things they used to when she lived at home. Bridgette couldn't wait, she felt excited and she needed the break. It had been exhausting!

Bridgette was amazed that Karen and Neil were actually taking time off work. Neil was still working from home. His workload was lighter in the summer months. He'd explained this was often the case with insurance because there were more problems during the winter months, burst pipes, floods or even global disasters! Neil now worked as an advisor for a firm of loss adjusters which dealt with property. Karen's holiday was the biggest surprise, because she'd said it was impossible to take time off. Bridgette noticed their weeks didn't overlap, so they wouldn't spend any time off together. Perhaps this was what people did when they had heavy schedules? It was sad to think that the children wouldn't have the benefit of both parents at the same time, during the school holidays! Bridgette was relieved to be going home where she would feel young again, at least for a few weeks. Surely eighteen-year-olds weren't supposed to ponder on difficult domestic situations. They should be out having fun, she thought, as she hastily packed her suitcase.

Neil was helpful and insisted on driving her all the way to Liverpool Street. He had an appointment In the City, later that day. It cut down her travelling time, and she was home in Suffolk within a couple of hours. Fortunately, the weather had changed for the better which was great because she loved the warm weather, and Bridgette planned to make the most of it. Her

Her parents were thrilled to see her. To make things even better, her mother had made her an eighteenth birthday cake, because they'd missed her birthday and she wanted to surprise her. Bridgette went into the kitchen to have a sneaky look. It looked delicious. It had been iced with white fondant icing and there were eighteen candles. There was also a lucky horseshoe in the middle with the words 'Good Luck on Your18th,' in gold. Bridgette's heart melted as she realised how much she'd missed her parents and being home. Without a word, she ran upstairs, flung herself on the bed and cried. Her tears came quickly. They were tears of exhaustion and frustration, and some were also about Neil. Bridgette went to get a large hanky. There were some old ones in a drawer, which still housed a few of her clothes. She wiped her eyes, blew her nose, then realised how silly she'd been about everything, especially Neil. If only she could change her thoughts, her life would be simple! She planned to go and meet her friends at eight o'clock at the Royal William. Fiona said she was coming with her which was great. They were going to have a family dinner first and then head off. The William was their local, and it was only a five-minute walk. It was fantastic to spend time with her sister. Bridgette felt so much better!

They were both in high spirits when they arrived at the pub, after eating birthday cake and drinking several glasses of champagne with their parents before they left!

'I'll buy the drinks,' declared Bridgette, who suddenly felt proud she was a working woman. 'What's everyone having?' she asked.

Bridgette's friends arrived in ones and twos until the only missing person was Mark. She felt a little relieved that he hadn't joined them and wondered if he was working. A few of them had gone away to work, like Jane, who worked in London. Sadly, she couldn't make it tonight. Bridgette missed Jane. She was her best friend, but they promised each other they'd have a night out in London when Bridgette was back in Surrey. Quite a few friends were still living at home, in the vicinity of the pub, so they'd walked.

'I love being eighteen', exclaimed Bridgette. She felt happy. No getting up early for a crazy routine. Her school days felt like a doddle but even the solicitor's office was easy compared to her nanny job. Still, she loved being a nanny and didn't want her life to change. Coming back to Suffolk gave her the best of both worlds. Having a car in Surrey gave her independence, and when she came back, she could have fun with her friends.

It was nearly nine o'clock, and the group had started to play pool. They had quickly formed into two teams, boys versus girls, which they'd done many times before. It was always fun, but then they realised there were only seven of them.

'Never mind, let's get going and see how it pans out. Mark said he wouldn't be here until ten because he's got a project to finish but when I told him, it was Bridgette's birthday, he said he'd definitely come,' Sharon told the group, which surprised Bridgette. Five minutes later after Mark had walked to the bar to get himself a drink, Bridgette suddenly noticed him take a shot and she was immediately surprised by his new-found confidence. He appeared to have changed significantly since she left. What had he been doing in her absence? Perhaps he'd been dating someone? No doubt he'd let her know after a few drinks, because he was hopeless at keeping secrets.

'Bridgette, I've missed you. It's so great to see you at last. Let me get you a drink, it's your birthday!' he said enthusiastically, as he moved towards her for a hug. Bridgette had already had three drinks since they'd arrived. All her friends wanted to spoil her because they hadn't seen her for months plus it was her birthday! She gratefully accepted the drinks then found she couldn't stop laughing. Her voice had become loud, but she couldn't change it. She was so pleased to be back with her friends, and it felt like yesterday since she saw them. It was proving to be a fun evening!

Why was she so drawn to Mark, she couldn't understand it? Perhaps, all she needed was for someone to put their arm around her. Coming home had made her so emotional, and she'd always felt safe with him, and tonight he looked so different, almost handsome! He appeared more mature in trousers and a shirt. He's obviously been spending some money on himself, she concluded. Why had she pushed him away so quickly, they could have stayed in touch. Had Mark been annoying or just familiar? Was knowing someone well, also comforting?

As the evening wore on, Bridgette became wobbly on her feet. She was having difficulty playing pool and decided to sit down. Fiona had her jacket on and was ready to leave.

'Come on, Bridgette, why don't we go home and get some sleep? We're going shopping early tomorrow!' she reminded her.

Bridgette was still laughing and having fun. The last thing she wanted to do was to be sensible. She was always sensible. She was born that way, it was boring. Every single day she'd been responsible for three children, and she felt like their mother. Right now, she wanted to be a normal reckless, eighteen-year-old.

'It's all right, Fiona, I'll take Bridgette home. I've got my car outside,' said Mark confidently.

Bridgette nodded to indicate things were ok. Then, one of the other girls decided to leave, so she could walk home with Fiona.

Twenty minutes later, Mark put his arm around Bridgette's shoulders which was something she thought would never happen again, and if it did, she'd hate it. But surprisingly, she enjoyed the comforting feeling of being close to him.

'Come on then, young lady. Let's take you home.'

Bridgette started to walk with Mark towards his car. He still had the same vehicle, an old bright yellow Ford Escort. She got into the seat beside him and closed the car door. Mark was already in the car and about to turn the keys when she had a compelling feeling to kiss him. She leaned across to his side of the vehicle and pulled his head gently towards hers as she slid her lips onto his. It wasn't long before he returned her kisses, thinking that Bridgette must have really missed him. As their kissing continued, Mark's hand slowly quickly slid over her knee and up her leg as he lifted her skirt. Bridgette began to feel a strange woozy sensation in her head and decided not to move around so quickly. She could also taste the earlier champagne in her mouth which made her feel sick.

'Oh, hang on a minute, Mark, what's the time?' Bridgette asked as she tried to gather her thoughts.

She was staying at her parents so, making herself too late wasn't a good idea?

'Quarter to eleven' answered Mark, as he continued to slide her skirt upwards with a little more determination.

'I think we better get out of this car park and go somewhere quieter,' whispered Bridgette, who wanted some fresh air.

'Down by the river?' suggested Mark.

The river was an old favourite of theirs, and it was only a ten-minute drive. Bridgette had often gone there with him for walks in the daytime but they'd never been there at night!

When they arrived, it was extremely dark, and they were the only people in the car park. Mark went to open the car door for Bridgette, but she was in no fit state to walk. Realising this, Mark drove the car right up to the edge of the trees on the boundary of the car park. He then started to wind his car seat down so that he was almost flat. Bridgette found that there was just enough room for her to climb onto his lap. She then stripped off her tee-shirt and began to kiss him. It wasn't long before they were having sex together. Bridgette was shocked by how quickly this happened, but she felt unable to prevent it. It was boiling in the car, but somehow, she reached her arm out to open the car window. Sweat started to stream down her face and the back of her neck which made her feel very uncomfortable. Bridgette suddenly became aware of the time. They'd been down by the river for over half an hour. She felt anxious and sick and clambered back into the passenger seat without saying a word. Her stomach felt churned up, and although she'd previously been enjoying herself, she now felt extremely deflated. She didn't know why her mood had changed so quickly, but she wanted to go home.

'Come on, let's get dressed,' she demanded as if she was talking to a child! 'It's now ten to twelve, and I promised Fiona I would be back by twelve. The William shuts at eleven thirty and Mum and Dad will be wondering where I am.'

Mark did up his zip and fastened his belt. He cleaned the window with a cloth to get rid of the condensation and started the engine. Bridgette couldn't understand why she had been enjoying herself one minute and then she suddenly felt flat. An out of control, panic began to rise in her, and she couldn't stop thinking about Neil. If only Mark was Neil, but they were so different. If she hadn't been so drunk, this would never have happened, she thought feeling angry at herself. An awkward silence soon developed between them, and Bridgette avoided Mark's gaze. She knew she had made a horrible mistake and talking was futile. As the car drew up outside her parents' house, she grabbed her handbag and gave Mark a quick peck on the cheek.

'I'll write,' Bridgette said, as she slammed the car door but she knew it was unlikely when she couldn't get Neil out of her head! It was only a few more weeks until she returned to Surrey, which was a relief. She was already fed up of Suffolk! Fortunately, her parents had gone to bed. They must have felt the effects of the champagne too, thought Bridgette. As she slowly tiptoed past Fiona's bedroom, she noticed her light was still on, but to her relief, Fiona didn't say a word! Bridgette quickly climbed into her old bed. The safe and happy bed, which she loved and snuggled under the covers. Tonight, was a bad dream and tomorrow it would be forgotten, she whispered as she fell into a deep relaxing sleep.

CHAPTER 15
HALLOWEEN

Karen was seldom at home. She spent most of her time at work, at a conference, or with her friends, so Bridgette rarely saw her in the evenings. The children were always lively after dinner and tonight of all nights, they were particularly tiring. 'It's Halloween, trick or treats', they shouted over and over.

Bridgette had quickly settled back into her work, with the family, after her summer break. She loved her job, and fitted in well. The children loved her, too, and were excited to see her back. Bridgette found it hard saying goodbye to her parents and sister, but she knew the weeks would fly by and it wouldn't be long until Christmas! She was going to be too busy to miss them because her job didn't give her any time to think!

'Treat,' replied Bridgette, hoping the children would leave it there.

'Yes, treat. Come out with us around the village. You've got to help us collect sweets and money. The other nanny did,' demanded Jonathan

'Sweets and money, do you think that's really a good idea? After all, it's freezing, and some people might not have much money, this time of year.'

'It's fine. We went last year, and we've got the clothes to dress up in, even Carmel's got a huge witch's hat!' said Jonathan.

So, it looked as if she was going to have to go, or the children would keep shouting forever. Bridgette had never done it before, but it was going to be fun being dressed up in a long black dress even if it had belonged to their previous nanny. She must have been quite a sport, thought Bridgette as she changed into the dress which appeared to be the right size!

It was freezing outside, but the neighbours appeared happy to donate a little money and sweets to the children. Most of them smiled at them, because they knew who they were, and a few chatted for a while and asked how she was getting on! Fortunately, they got around all the nearby houses in an hour, and they were soon glad to be back in the warm, with their buckets full. Once they had some hot soup inside them, the children continued to shout and tear around the house, not wanting to slow down. They screamed about ghosts, vampires and superman! Don't they ever get tired, she muttered because she was desperate to sit down and relax. Eventually they calmed down a little after their bedtime drinks and biscuits, and they took themselves to bed. The children had been upstairs for about fifteen minutes when Carmel started shouting, 'I'm frightened, I need a story, story' until she was very loud. Bridgette wearily climbed the stairs and sat in her usual place at the side of her bed and started to read her one of her favourite books. Not long now, she thought, and I'll be able to have some time to myself. I need my dinner, and then I'll probably go straight to bed!

It was at this point that Bridgette heard the front door bang. She guessed it was either Karen or Neil coming in from work, so she quickly waved goodnight to Carmel and quietly closed her bedroom door. Thankfully, the child was almost asleep, so Bridgette tiptoed away slowly. It must have been all that trick and treating, she's completely worn out! The witch's hat, which had been way too large, sat at the end of her bed. Bridgette laughed. Carmel must have been the smallest witch her neighbours had ever seen. Surprisingly she had really enjoyed herself.

Bridgette opened the door to the kitchen, thinking it might be Karen, but it was Neil, and he was already preparing his dinner.

'Hi, are you making your own dinner tonight?' she asked, as she watched Neil fetch a large saucepan from the cupboard.

'Yes, Karen will be very late tonight. She's going out after work with some girlfriends, a hen night or something. How about you? Are you going out, it's Halloween? Have you tried the local pub yet, there must be something going on there?' Neil asked, sounding quite jovial.

'No, not yet, but I will soon, I'm shattered. I took the children out to trick and treat, and it wore them out. They've only just settled down because they went a little wild afterwards. It was hard to calm them down!'

'Oh really, I think the previous Nanny did that with them, and found the same! She was great with them, but you know how to weave a special kind of magic! Yes, I'm cooking tonight, fish pie. You're quite welcome to have some with me, and I've got a nice bottle of white wine we could share.'

'Brilliant, that sounds great,' replied Bridgette, who was thrilled at having a meal cooked for her. What a relief she thought, when she finally sat down.

Bridgette watched Neil prepare the fish pie. She offered to help, but he knew how tired she was and he told her to sit down. He enjoyed cooking. As she watched, he told her a bit more about his work and Karen's job. He went into great detail about his insurance business! He didn't ask much about the children, but he seemed pleased to hear that they'd gone to bed.

'Everyone spoils them rotten' he jested with his captivating smile. Bridgette couldn't help but admire Neil's good looks. His face was beginning to show a few lines, but rather than old, it just made him look intelligent. I would imagine he gets what he wants most of the time, she thought, even in business!

When Neil talked about his art, Bridgette noticed his whole face light up.

'I think your paintings are great. I love the bold colours and the way you capture the surf,' said Bridgette.

'That's down to many hours of watching. The best time to go to the beach is very early in the morning when the sun hits the top of the water, there's nothing better. You would imagine by looking at the sea, that the waves break in an orderly fashion, but really, it's mayhem. It's a bit like life, each wave being at a different stage of development, yet being as important as the next. There are small waves that just ripple onto the beach, and large waves that have such strength you marvel at their power. The whole thing just blows you away.' 'It's ready now?' said Neil as he turned his attention to the dinner. Bridgette thought the fish pie looked delicious. He was obviously a good cook, and she thought it a shame that he didn't cook more often!

Bridgette and Neil sat together, at the small pine table, in the corner of the large kitchen. They were opposite because there wasn't enough room for both of them, side by side. This was the table where Bridgette fed the children during the day, and it was small. She was surprised that Neil or Karen even used it, but it was convenient.

When the pie was gone, they sat for a while, chatting and drinking. Bridgette didn't usually drink wine because she preferred lager, apart from when she went home! She noticed that this wine was strong and the level of the bottle quickly dropped until there was just one glass left.

'Final glass?' inquired Neil and Bridgette nodded her head in reply. She felt light-headed, but she enjoyed the feeling. Everything Neil said, was funny, and their conversation was very light-hearted. She knew he was teasing her, but she loved it. He was somewhere between a father figure, and a friend, but despite this, she felt something else between them which was hard to put her finger on. Bridgette suddenly became aware that Neil's knee was touching hers under the table. Was he doing it deliberately, or was the table just small, and his legs long? Whatever the reason, it was an enjoyable sensation, and she moved her legs slightly closer to him. Neil's knee was now pressed up against hers, and she could feel shivers running through her body. Their contact fueled her physical attraction to him, and she was frozen to the spot. She knew it would be better to get up, make an excuse and leave, or to turn on the television, but she was captivated by this man and she couldn't help but enjoy the attention. Then, at last, Neil broke the silence. 'Would you like to put the kettle on, Bridgette? We could do with some coffee to sober up.' Bridgette was relieved that Neil said this, and she forced herself to move towards the sink to fill the kettle. Her back was to him as she switched it on. All of a sudden, Bridgette felt a sturdy pair of arms around her waist, as his body pressed against her. His lips were also in her hair and moving down her neck, giving her tender kisses. Bridgette stood motionless. Could this be happening? Her logical mind wanted to push him away, but her body told her differently. She didn't want to move or say anything to Neil because she was enjoying the sensations spreading through her. Neil took his hands away from her waist and spread them over her breasts, as he cupped and fondled her, he whispered, 'I want you, Bridgette, you know that, don't you? I've wanted you for weeks. Don't you remember our walk in the woods together? I wanted to kiss you then. I've seen you looking at me, and haven't you been thinking about us?'

Bridgette turned to face Neil. Her face was very close to his. 'I have been thinking about you Neil, but I can't. It isn't right. What about Karen? Will you tell her because I don't want to lose my job!'

'Don't worry about that. I don't tell Karen everything. You're safe with me.'

Neil leaned forward and pressed his lips hard onto her mouth, which opened to accept his kiss. Her arms automatically slid around his neck so that she could feel his hair with her outstretched fingers. Then he took her hand in his and led her out of the kitchen, towards the foot of the stairs. 'We'll have to be quiet because of the children but don't worry, we have loads of time. Karen won't be home for hours, if at all!' he said, looking into her eyes deeply.

Bridgette could hardly hear Neil's voice because her head was whirling, her heart was pounding, and her throat was too dry to speak. She knew that if she climbed the stairs it was consent to whatever lay ahead, but why worry about the future? The only thing that mattered to her now was an overwhelming feeling of excitement. It was true, she did want Neil as much as he wanted her, so was there any point in resisting?

CHAPTER 16
SETTLING IN

As the weeks passed, Bridgette found she was cheerful in this home. She loved the children and got on well with Karen. Although nothing more had happened with Neil, Bridgette knew he was still attracted to her because he often gave her sideways glances, winks or knowing smiles. But there was very little time for them to spend time alone together, not in the way that Bridgette wanted. She felt sure that if the opportunity arose, Neil would let her know, and she had to be content with that!

It was now the end of November and the children were already beginning to talk about Christmas. 'Not yet,' she kept telling them. 'It's far too early for Christmas songs or paper decorations. We'll have plenty of time for that, in December.' The children found it difficult to keep calm, and there was a real feeling of excitement in the air. Then one evening, after their tea, while she was watching her usual soap, the telephone rang.

'It's for you Bridgette, I think it's one of your friends.' call Karen.

Bridgette raced into the hallway to pick up the phone. She hadn't heard from any of her friends for months, so she was excited and surprised to discover it was Jane! Great, thought Bridgette, at last, now we can have some fun. It was about time because she really missed being with her friends, especially her.

'Hi Bridgette, it's been so long. What have you been up to? You've been hiding away for months; we've got to get together soon! Can you make Saturday night?

'Yes, get me out of here! I don't care where we go as long as we have fun. I need some adult company. I love talking to children, but it's starting to do my head in.' Bridgette whispered.

'Ok, then, get the tube into the city and I'll meet you at Covent Garden. We'll go to the jazz café I told you about. It was great last time, everyone just lost their inhibitions after a few glasses of wine and danced. You'll love it, Bridgette. It's over eighteen, so we won't have to worry about kids getting in,' Jane explained.

Bridgette felt sure she'd have a great time with Jane, she always had in the past. She was smiling when she put down the phone.

'Going out?' asked Karen with interest.

'Yes, Saturday night, if that's all right with you?'

'Of course. I'm pleased you're having fun at last.'

Bridgette rushed up to her bedroom. She was really excited, but her head was swimming for some reason. It had done this a few times lately, but she thought it was probably just tiredness or the start of a bug.

'I'm going to have to take a rest' she shouted to Karen from the stairs.

'Fine, Bridgette. I'm here to look after the children tonight, so I'll get them ready for bed. Thanks for your help today.'

Karen said this nearly every day, to Bridgette. She was very good at saying thank you and Bridgette felt appreciated, which made her feel guilty about her behaviour with Neil! She decided to try not to think about it because it was unlikely to happen again. It was just a one-off. Neil appeared to be a man of his word, and their secret was safe. Right now, it was more important to decide what to wear

Bridgette took some clothes from her wardrobe and spread them on her bed. She wanted to try them all on because Jane always looked great and she wanted to look her best. After not seeing her for so long, she knew Jane must have changed. As she took her make-up out of her bedside table, Bridgette suddenly realised that she'd forgotten to take her contraceptive pill this morning which alarmed her because this had never happened before. It was never a problem when she was with Mark but then she didn't have so much to think about. The last packet appeared empty but she then noticed that she'd forgotten to take three pills in a row. The tablets were in the middle of the last month. Hang on a minute, she thought racing over to the calendar.

It must have been over Halloween, when she had slept with Neil, but why worry when she felt fine. Her imagination was definitely getting the better of her. The exhaustion she felt was due to the children, nothing else. Working as a nanny was hard work and too much responsibility!

* * * * * * * *

Bridgette woke suddenly and realised it was Saturday. Fortunately, she was able to lay in bed a little longer this morning and catch up on sleep. She looked at the clock, then drifted back off for a couple of hours. She emerged around ten, but despite all the extra sleep, she still felt tired. What was the matter with her? Maybe taking a shower would liven her up. She wanted to feel excited about seeing Jane, but for some reason, she didn't because she didn't feel herself this morning. The pains in her stomach continued. It must be my period coming on she concluded as she raced into her toilet to be sick. Then a horrible feeling came over her. Was she pregnant? How could she be? Her period was just late. She looked at her packets of pills again and ran her fingers over the few she'd forgotten. She couldn't deal with this. If by chance she was, what would she do? The odds of that happening were slim. It would wreck her life and ruin everything. She'd have to go back home to her parents and that would be terrible. Bridgette's mind raced, but deep down she knew she'd have to take the test bought from the local chemist yesterday, when she started to fee iffy! It couldn't be put it off any longer. Surely it was too early for a result, but after reading the instructions for the second time, it appeared that you could have a result ten days after your missed period was due. Bridgette's hands were shaking so much, it felt impossible, but at last she managed to dip the gadget into some urine. If she was pregnant, it would show a thin blue within three minutes. She decided the best thing was to leave her bedroom to get a cup of tea. After all, it was most likely that she'd caught something from the children, they were always complaining of tummy aches, which drove her mad!

'Good morning, Bridgette' said Neil as he looked up from his daily newspaper, but Bridgette was definitely not in the mood to talk. She mumbled hi, and quickly grabbed some coffee. There was only one minute to go, and her hands were still shaking.

'Are you looking forward to tonight? Karen told me that you are going to meet some friends in the city. A jazz bar or something?' he continued.

Bridgette forced herself to reply.

'Yes, it'll be great. I'm looking to seeing my friend Jane and having a bit of a sing-song.'

'A sing-song! I didn't know you liked that sort of thing. I would have put you down as a Duran Duran fan?'

Bridgette looked at her watch and realised the test would be ready.

'Well, I'm full of surprises!' she replied, and then vanished!

'Oh no, I don't believe it. This is too much!' She shook the tube violently to see if the blue would go away, but it was staying! How could she be? It was impossible through having sex with a man once. Was that even possible? Although, deep in her heart, Bridgette knew it was, and she'd been unlucky! She quickly opened her bedroom window to inhale the November air. Condensation started to run down the inside, so she quickly closed it so the wall didn't get damp. Her head was spinning continuously with crazy thoughts, which made her giddy. What would she say to Karen or more to the point what would she tell Neil? Her life here was finished when she was just starting to enjoy herself! She'd have to go home, and that was the last thing she wanted to do right now! What choice did she have? She would no longer be able to carry on working as a nanny. Maybe she could just pretend nothing had happened? That could be the answer, at least for now. I would give her the chance to speak to Neil in private. Perhaps, he'd suggest a solution, so she could stay. How could she handle this alone? She'd keep quiet about it for now and if she needed to tell someone, then she'd tell Jane. Jane was very supportive and she was bound to help. In the meantime, there was tonight to contend with even if it no longer felt like fun!

CHAPTER 17
HAVING FUN

Bridgette walked over to her wardrobe and took out a black dress with a plunging neckline which finished just above the knee. It looked a little plain, so she tied a silky gold scarf around her neck and put on some long dangle earrings. The dangly earrings sparkled with fake diamonds which gave her a glamorous appearance. She looked much older than her years. She decided to have a really great night with Jane. Whatever had happened this morning felt like a dream but it was something she could deal with at a later stage. It wasn't worth worrying about now, because tonight she was having fun.

It was dark outside, and the packed tube swung around the bends, which made Bridgette feel uncomfortable. She couldn't see much through the windows because her vision was obscured by so many people, plus she had to keep her eye on the wall map to follow her route. The Piccadilly line was jam-packed, so Bridgette counted the stations in her head as the tube neared Covent Garden. When there were two stations to go, she began to feel excited about her night out. Standing opposite her was a young woman who appeared in her early twenties, with a buggy. The child in the pushchair was sucking a dummy, and his big brown eyes looked up at Bridgette, which made her smile. The mother didn't have a seat, so she had to stand, holding on to the rail with one hand and the buggy with the other. Bridgette was lucky enough to find a seat and wondered whether to give it up, but it was too difficult to push her way over there!

That will be me in a year thought Bridgette as the memory of the morning came flooding back. Was having this baby her only option? Surely, there was another choice. Unfortunately, the other choices were something she couldn't bear to think about. She'd take a look at the options in a few weeks when things were clearer. Still deep in thought, Bridgette suddenly realised it was the place to get off, and she pushed her way to the sliding door.

Jane was waiting for her on the platform. She also wore a short dress which looked fabulous. It appeared to be made of some silky green material and her blonde hair, which usually rested on her shoulders, had been raised into a pile with various clips and beads to secure it in place. Jane's make-up glittered in the evening light, and Bridgette was amazed to see how sophisticated and happy she looked.

'You look fabulous,' exclaimed Bridgette.

'Well, take a look at you!' answered Jane, returning her compliment.

'Oh, and I've got a surprise for you. You are going to meet my new boyfriend, Phillip, you'll love him. He used to be in the forces, but I've also invited one of his friends so you'll have someone to dance with,' Jane blurted out excitedly. Everything seemed to come rushing out in one breath which Bridgette found a little overwhelming.

Bridgette was unsure about this. She was still feeling a little sick from being swung around on the tube, and now she had to cope with meeting someone new and making conversation!

'Does he like talking about children? You did tell him I'm a nanny and do nothing but read children's' stories and play games all day?'

'I think he'd like the playing games, but I'm not sure that he's after a bedtime story. He might be!' replied Jane, jokingly. Bridgette also laughed then remembered it was always fun with Jane. Fortunately, they were meeting inside the jazz bar, which gave them a little time to catch up before the men arrived. As they approached the bar, Bridgette noticed two fairly tall men waiting outside the front of the venue. As they walked up, the good-looking Phillip suddenly popped his arm around Jane's shoulders.

'Hello I'm Phillip, and this is Sean, spelt the Irish way, the same way as in Sean Connery! Actually, Sean is Irish, and he's got the sense of humour to go with it, haven't you? I'm sure you two will get on great,' Phillip said, giving him a little push towards Bridgette.

Bridgette was pleasantly surprised. Sean wasn't at all what she imagined. In front of her stood a well-built, good-looking guy with dark hair, wearing a red opened necked, shirt. His face was slightly weathered as if he had worked outside for a few years.

'Sean has done a bit of everything. He's a master at driveways and playing the fiddle at weddings. I expect he'll tell you all about it. We work together in the insurance business. I'm his senior at the moment,' Phillip explained, suddenly pulling rank. It was apparent to Bridgette that this was just banter to impress the ladies. Most of the conversation that followed was about who was the best at attracting new business, and Bridgette found it dull. To make things worse, the word 'insurance,' reminded her of Neil. As the evening went on, she surprisingly warmed to 'Mr Connery'. He definitely had a touch of rugged charm about him. Bridgette felt this was a strange combination. One she'd never encountered before, but nevertheless, it was attractive. He also had very sparkly eyes that drew her into his conversation. She loved his little jokes, which she could relate to because they were roughly the same age. When he got to an old story about an Irishman, Scotsman and Englishman, Bridgette teased him.

'Not that old joke again!' she sighed, but she continued to laugh and to her surprise, she was really enjoying herself.

'Well, tell me your story then, Bridgette. What do you do?' blurted Sean, who suddenly brought her into the present.

'I know you and Jane went to school together, in Suffolk but I don't know anything else about you. Don't let me do all the talking. The Irish are good at that,' he said, with a grin.

'My job isn't that interesting,' started Bridgette, who didn't want to talk about it.

'I can't see a nice young lady like you being boring. Are you telling me porky pies?' Sean jested.

'I'm a traffic warden,' Bridgette declared. She didn't want to discuss Neil or Karen and she had to get through tonight somehow. She'd worry about the rest of her life when she got home but tonight was meant

A to be fun!

'If you're a traffic warden, then I'm James Bond. Nice to meet you, Miss Spend a Penny,' whispered Sean mimicking Sean Connery.

Bridgette accidentally dropped her guard, and for the first time in months, she began to laugh. When she began laughing, it was impossible to stop.

'Let's have a dance,' said Sean, after they'd finished their meal.

Several glasses of wine later, Bridgette began to let her hair down and she decided to dance with him. They smooched to old Frank Sinatra songs. The pianist also played some traditional jazz, Ella Fitzgerald, Bessie Smith and other popular tunes. As he banged on the piano, the notes became louder, and the sound filled her ears. Bridgette was taken by the moment and suddenly snuggled up to Sean without thinking. To her relief, she forgot all about Neil and the baby growing inside her

CHAPTER 18
SISTER MARY'S BIRTHDAY

It was Sister Mary's sixtieth birthday, and only a month until Christmas. She sat at a little table, in the kitchen, writing Christmas cards and letters to her friends, so that they'd arrive before Christmas. Mary made many acquaintances over the years, and some of the cards were for the girls who had stayed at St. Catherine's, while others were for the nuns who had worked with her. A few of them said they wanted to keep in touch with her, which she thought a blessing. Mary also sent cards to her family. She'd tried to stay in touch with them for years, despite never receiving a response. There hadn't been a single card or letter from her since she joined St. Catherine's, forty years ago. She wondered if her parents were still alive but decided to send cards anyway in the hope that maybe, one day, things would change. Mary knew she was an entirely different person to the girl who lived with her family. The past no longer felt part of her life. Everything had become a distant memory with no-one to remind her of her childhood.

Mary felt a mixture of both joy and sadness today because next week, she would be leaving St Catherine's. She had been given permission to work more within the community which she was extremely happy about. Her accommodation would still be in grounds and she'd been allocated a small cottage, near the main gate. Things would be different because she'd have more time for gardening and other things that she'd missed over the years.

Mary was content in many ways, but she sometimes wondered how things would have been if she had been blessed with a husband and children. She knew that it was probably for the best that her life had turned out the way it had because her work had brought her close to God. If she'd stayed at a very strict convent, her life could have been awful, so she counted her blessings. When her situation changed, she planned to grow roses because she adored flowers. There were also sewing projects to finish and she also wanted to try water colour painting, which until recently she considered impossible. They were always so busy. Her arthritis appeared to be worsening, that's why she'd sought permission to work within the community instead of working with the babies. Her new work involved fundraising, and she could work her own hours. Mary was really looking forward to the change and continuing in whatever way she could. It was all God's work.

Today, there was the matter of the correspondence, which had continued to pile up since Margaret's departure. Mary felt it was a chore having to answer so many letters. Most of them were from social workers and adoption societies. The amount they received was unbelievable. What a nightmare the change in the law had created. Surely it wasn't their job to reconcile parents and children, there must be other organisations for that!

Mary sometimes thought about the letter she found on that dreadful day, when Margaret was ill. Was it her Gillian, who had grown to be a successful businesswoman? She realised she may never be entirely sure if this lady were her child but she wanted to think of her that way because it kept the memory of her baby alive. Her daughter was now grown-up and married and adopting a child herself! If only she had a photograph of her. Her mind was confused, and she felt emotional. It had proved impossible to confront Margaret because her illness had quickly developed into pneumonia, and she'd died a few weeks later. Mary knew her secret would never be revealed unless she wrote to Gillian's family. It did feel the right to tell them about Margaret's death. It might also be her only chance to discover the truth! However, there was a part of her that thought if God had intended it to be this way, it was better left alone. Digging up the past was for the young and it was time that she was left in peace.

Despite being Mary's birthday, she still had her routine work to do and she treated it like any other day. It started by her going through the mail. The first letter in the pile that caught her attention was from a young woman called Bridgette, which was addressed to the Reverend Mother, as most of them were!

Dear Reverend Mother,

I'm writing to inquire whether if you have any news about my mother. I understand from my parents, she came to St Catherine's in July 1962. I have an urgent reason for wanting to talk to her. I have tried to trace her for a very long time, but I was told that you need to be eighteen and I was eighteen this summer. I'm desperate to talk to her because I'm in a similar position myself. I would like to come to St. Catherine's to speak to someone about my adoption. I don't know what to do. I understand that St Catherine's is still open? Do you still arrange adoptions? I will be returning to live with my parents shortly, but I don't know what I want. It will be difficult for me to keep the baby because I'm a nanny, and I want to return to my job. In the meantime, any information you can supply me about my mother would help. I understand from my parents that she was called Rebecca O'Brien and her home address was somewhere in East London. Please help me. I will leave my telephone number at the top of this letter so that someone can telephone me.

Kind Regards
Bridgette Woods

Mary re-read the letter. She didn't remember many of the girl's names and Rebecca was quite a common name. Although, having a surname, month and year helped. Girls often looked for their parents and discovered that they hadn't even stayed at St. Catherine's. They were just desperate to get in touch with anyone who could help. As for getting in contact with Rebecca, well, that might prove to be tricky. A letter could be written on Bridgette's behalf, but it would be better if she discussed it with a social worker first. It wasn't her job to advise her. She could only point her in the right direction. Now the adoption laws had changed things were difficult. There were more rules around who was allowed to do what! Mary knew of cases where children just turned up on their parents' doorstep, without a second thought. They assumed it was their right to be in their lives, and they didn't think of the consequences.

Sister Mary was tired of this. It was so draining. All she wanted to do was to plant roses in her new little garden and not pulled into any more problems. After all, next week was fast approaching then she could, at last, have a well-earned rest. So, if Bridgette were coming, it would have to be quick. Mary thought that it was unlikely she'd be replaced because there wasn't the funding. Unofficially she knew that St. Catherine's would close soon. The home didn't take many babies now, in the days of abortions. If Bridgette wanted to give her baby up for adoption, it would make a couple extremely happy but she'd need to refer her to another agency. Mary thought it was odd she would wish to do this, especially now, when single parents generally kept their children. After a long deep sigh, Mary decided there was no time like the present and she'd try and get Bridgette on the telephone. Her number was scribbled in the letter.

Bridgette was sitting down in a chair having a quick cup of tea when the telephone rang. She'd given Sister Mary the house phone number which wasn't ideal, but she had little choice.

'Hello, who's that?' Bridgette asked suspiciously, not recognising the voice on the other end of the line. Fortunately, she was alone when the phone rang. Neil and Karen were still at work, and the children were watching television programs before their tea.

'Hello, Bridgette, It's Sister Mary from St. Catherine's. I received your letter and I wondered if you wanted to come here for a chat? If you want to come, then it might be better sooner than later, because I won't be working here much longer. If you want to find out about your mother, I'm afraid it will have to be quick. Strictly speaking, you should have gone through one of the adoption society's social workers and not approached us directly.

The children started to look bored and Carmel ran up the stairs to show off.

'Quiet, please! I'm on the telephone. Stop squabbling over the channels,' Bridgette hissed in a loud whisper. Finally, they got the message, and Carmel returned downstairs and settled down again with Jonathon and Lucy.

Bridgette couldn't believe it! She hadn't expected a response from St. Catherine's that quickly. Perhaps they have some information regarding her mother's whereabouts? She'd thought about her mother for years, and now the time had finally come. It felt surreal. It would be incredible if she made contact with her. There she was pregnant, going to be a mother and she wanted to search for her own birth mother. It had felt like the right time. The logical side of her brain said, why would you want to do this? And the emotional part of her said there were many unanswered questions that she needed to the answers to.

Neil and Karen would be home soon. For once, they were actually coming home together. I'm going to have to tell someone about all this, she whispered out loud. I can't handle it all on my own. She hoped a meeting with Sister Mary would give her the help she needed.

'Are you still there, Bridgette? I can fit you in early next week. How about Tuesday, in the afternoon, one o'clock?'

'I'll have to find out if I can take a day off work, but I'm sure that will be fine.' replied Bridgette decisively. There was no point in putting it off when she was desperate for answers. By finding her own mother, Bridgette hoped it would be easier to make a decision about her own life. She also decided to phone Jane later and tell her the truth.

Bridgette waited until the children were in bed and Karen and Neil had closed the front door to go out for the evening. They were taking the MG. But she was unsure where they were going because Neil had just said they would be two or three hours and Karen was carrying a bottle of wine!

'You're what! Are you sure Bridgette? You're probably wrong,' replied Jane, later that evening.

'No, I'm not wrong, Jane. My period was late, so I took a test. I've been sick every morning, and I don't need to ask a doctor to check, because I know,' added Bridgette. She was crying down the phone to Jane, but she also felt relieved that she'd told her. It took the weight off her shoulders, and she felt lighter.

'Bridgette, if you're going to keep this baby, you'll have to let Mark know, and you'll have to go home to your parents. Although, you could always stay with me for a while until you and Mark are settled.'

Mark, thought Bridgette. She thinks Mark's the father! It was on the tip of her tongue to say, 'actually it isn't Mark's baby,' when she stopped herself. Perhaps that was the answer. It was dreadful to lie to Jane, but she didn't have a choice!

'No, don't worry. I'll tell him soon. I'm going back to Suffolk for Christmas, so I can speak to him then,' she replied a little more positively.

'Well, I guess that's the end to our nights out in London. It's a pity because we had great fun last Saturday and I know that Sean liked you. He was hoping to do it again. Maybe we could all go and see a film together. He doesn't need to know you're pregnant. We could still have fun.'

Bridgette suddenly felt sad, what had she done? Surely, she should be out having fun with her friends, instead of worrying about keeping a roof over her head? Her life was rapidly turning into a nightmare. It was ironic because she'd enjoyed herself that night with Jane, and Sean was far more fun than expected.

Oh Neil, if you only knew the mess we created, thought Bridgette, When, their phone call was over, she wanted to sob her heart out, but the children needed to be looked after. After dabbing her eyes, they appeared a little better. At least the meeting was arranged, which was a step forward.

* * * * * * * *

It was eleven pm, and Bridgette turned off the television. It was something to do to pass the time, and the late-night chat show was over. She'd began to wonder about locking the back door when she suddenly heard it open and someone walk in. At last, she could go to bed, knowing they were back home. As she walked into the hallway, she expected to see Karen and Neil together, but surprisingly, Neil was on his own.

'Where's Karen? I stayed up later because I thought you'd forgotten your keys. Look, there's a set still hanging on the hook?' asked Bridgette.

'Ah, they belong to Karen, I've got mine here. Karen isn't coming home tonight, so you could have gone to bed, sorry! We had a bit of a row, and she stomped off. She's just called to say that she's staying at her girlfriend's flat in the city, tonight.'

'Oh dear', replied Bridgette. But she wasn't surprised because they were always arguing lately and she pretended not to notice because it made her feel awkward. To Bridgette's surprise, Neil continued, 'well, that's enough about us. What's the matter with you, young lady? You look as if you've been crying? Not boyfriend problems, I hope?'

'No, not boyfriend problems. I've been feeling a little unwell, lately.' She was surprised that he noticed.

'Ah, Dr Neil to the rescue,' he jested. 'Perhaps we need another day out?'

He's obviously has had too much to drink, she thought, feeling a little annoyed. Dr Neil, if only he could fix this problem!

'How about I make us both a nice cuppa and you can tell me about it?' he said, walking into the kitchen.

Bridgette followed Neil and sat down at the little table. She couldn't help but think about the last time they sat there. Bridgette wanted to tell him the whole story, but it didn't feel like the right time with him being slightly drunk. Despite feeling irritated by him, she still found him attractive! Would she always be attracted to him? What was the matter with her? Neil casually slipped an arm around her shoulders and hugged her close, and to her surprise, they were soon kissing. Oh no, I can't do this again she thought but her whole body said otherwise.

CHAPTER 19
HAPPIER DAYS

It was Tuesday and a very grey day indeed, and Mary was counting the days until Friday when at last, she would have some time to herself. There were still the usual jobs to be done this morning, admin, checking equipment, ordering supplies, visiting the wards and making sure there were no problems. Then, this afternoon, there was seeing health visitors and appointments with social workers. Her to-do list just went on and on, and at one o'clock, there was an appointment with Bridgette Woods. Mary had a full line up. By the end of the day, she knew that she would be on her knees! Still, thankfully, it was not for much longer. She enjoyed her work, but as the years wore on, Mary yearned for more freedom. She'd missed being able to do simple things like walking to the local shop to buy a newspaper, or doing a crossword, or spending a bit more time listening to music. Mary loved classical music, especially Mozart. There were so many classical concerts she would have attended if things had been different. Fortunately, things were changing and soon, she thought crossing another day off her calendar.

* * * * * * * * * *

Bridgette quickly jumped out of bed. Today was the day she'd dreamed about since she was a little girl. The day she'd discover more about her birth mother. There was plenty of time because her appointment with Sister Mary wasn't until one o'clock and, it was still early. To her relief her morning sickness had ebbed a little and over the last week, Bridgette had started to feel quite well. She felt a strange mixture of excitement and anticipation about today because she wanted to find out more about her adoption, but she was also scared. Hopefully, understanding her own circumstances would bring clarity to her life. Perhaps she'd discovered some answers already since she became aware of a strong maternal instinct. Her heart emanated a feeling that she could only describe as peaceful! It felt as if love flowed through the cells of her body directly to her child. Despite her difficulties, she didn't feel threatened by the outside world, which had, at times felt mean and cruel. In her short life, she had fought her way through many challenging situations and here was another one, but this felt different. Her natural instinct told her it was right to protect her baby because they were peaceful. It was the outside world which was wrong. Bridgette was suddenly angry at Neil and mad at herself. Why did this have to happen now, at the start of her career? Surely, if there were a God, he'd be here for her to help her decide what to do? But all she heard was silence. She'd even tried to pray and find answers within, but it was difficult. Please, God, show me where to go from here? It was frustrating. Perhaps Sister Mary would help her find the answers?

The morning passed quickly, with tidying her room and sorting out bits of washing, that she hadn't had time to do for weeks. When it came to midday, Bridgette made her way to the local bus stop. St. Catherine's was only five miles away from their home, but she didn't want to be late, so she'd allowed an hour to get there.

It was cold, and for the first time this year, Bridgette wore her long black coat, gloves, knee-high boots, with a skirt and jumper underneath. She didn't want to give the appearance of looking overdressed, but she had to keep warm. A gold cross, a gift from her parents, on her seventh birthday hung around her neck. It was a gift from them on her first Holy Communion. Bridgette wore the cross because she thought it would help her feel closer to God. The same questions kept going over and over in her mind. Did her mother want to give her up, or was she forced into it? Can you really move on with your life after giving up a child? Did her mother bond ever with her? There were so many questions, and some of them she knew Sister Mary would be unable to answer. They were all about her mother. She wasn't interested in her father, that would be too much. One step at a time thought Bridgette, as she got on to the bus.

Bridgette looked out of the windows. The family lived in a lovely area; she hadn't seen this part of town. There were many beautiful houses and old established trees. The bus regularly stopped to let people on and off. Families were carrying shopping bags, although a few people were obviously on their way to work. Neil and Karen had agreed to let her have the day off. She'd had so little time off since working for them, they were more than happy to oblige.

'Of course, you can Bridgette. Are you going anywhere special?' Karen had asked.

Bridgette hadn't wanted to say. She knew from experience that if she talked about her adoption, she'd become emotional. Now with her pregnancy, she felt even more up and down. Until she'd made a decision, it was important to keep it to herself.

'No, not really, I thought I'd visit some of the local villages and have lunch out.'

'Great' she replied, but Karen was only half listening because she was in a huge rush to sort out her paperwork. She packed her briefcase and headed to the front door, then shouted 'have a great time,' and that was it.

Bridgette soon found herself walking up a very long leafy driveway lined with hedges and rhododendron bushes. There were several tall trees, but they weren't nearly as tall as the pines in the forest she'd visited with Neil. There were oak trees, ash, beech and a few beautiful maples which merged displaying various shades of brown and yellow. The red leaves looked stunning. This had a very grounding effect on her, and she stomped her feet on the ground like a child. As the fallen leaves crunched under her feet, she started to gently kick them into the air, raising them about six inches or so to reveal the soft damp mud underneath. Bridgette breathed in the country air and she started to feel better. Thank goodness she was off that crowded bus. I'm sure Sister Mary can't be that much of an ogre, she thought quickening her pace.

St. Catherine's was a red-brick Victorian monstrosity. As architecture went it was no piece of art. The windows which were long and tall appeared to have been replaced quite a few years ago, but they looked out of place and gave it a hostile appearance. Bridgette didn't know much about buildings but guessed they were fifties windows with metal frames. The paintwork was cracked and peeling, and the glass dirty. The building looked more like a factory than a home. Various bricks had crumbled, and green moss and ivy were climbing randomly over large sections of the front of the house which appeared to need a lot of maintenance.

Bridgette walked towards a separate building, which had been added to the side of the main one, which was probably built the same time as the windows were changed. It contained a few decorated windows; the type Bridgette had seen in a church. As she approached the massive oak door, she saw a sizeable brass knocker with a separate bell. Bridgette pushed the doorbell as hard as she could, through her thick gloves, then shot back in surprise at the sound of the buzzer. She then stood back so her feet were resting on the gravelled drive and took some deep breaths to calm herself. Sometimes it did the trick, and other times it made her heart race even more!

Bridgette's hand went to her neck. She was pleased she was wearing her gold cross because it made her feel safe. After what seemed an age, Sister Mary opened the door to reveal a black and white tiled entrance porch. This was sizeable and contained several chairs and what appeared to be an old bench covered with the sort of magazines to be found in a Doctor's Surgery.

Sister Mary was a small, little plump lady with round wire-rimmed glasses. Her habit was a complete surprise to Bridgette being short and royal blue. She wasn't at all as Bridgette imagined. The Sister also wore a pair of everyday black shoes and tights. Her hair was covered by a white band that obscured most of her forehead. Bridgette was immediately surprised to find her smiling, and she started to warm to her.

'Come this way, my dear. It's warm in my office. St. Catherine's is such a rambling old building, it's hard to keep it warm nowadays. We only heat the rooms we use because we rely on donations. The sister opened the door to her office. It was a small room with the long-pointed cathedral type windows which Bridgette had surveyed from outside. The room was light and relatively pleasant with a large crucifix on the wall behind the desk, but apart from that, the walls were plain with a range of antique cupboards. There was also a vase of autumn flowers that stood on top of an old chest of drawers.

Bridgette sat down on a chair and gazed out of the window to the colourful trees beyond. Mary asked her a lot of questions and she began to talk about Mark, her job as a nanny, the children and also Neil. Sister Mary listened intently without interruption. When Bridgette finished, she spoke.

'So, let's run through this again,' she said, and started to scribble in a notebook. 'I hope you don't mind me keeping notes, but I've been having trouble remembering things lately. Rest assured anything you say, is confidential. I'll do all that I can to help you Bridgette, but you must understand I'll still have to seek permission from the adoption society. They'll probably send a social worker to your home.

'You're only six weeks pregnant, and you don't want an abortion. You are considering adoption, but you want to keep in contact with your child if your adoption is agreed,' repeated Sister Mary.

Bridgette realised that Mary must have heard similar stories many times before because she seemed quite 'matter of a fact,' which unnerved her. Did she really want to part with her baby?

'That's right,' Bridgette mumbled.

'You don't want the father of the baby, Neil, isn't it, to know about your pregnancy because he's your employer and he already has three children?'

'I also want some information about my mother,' replied Bridgette, who was desperate to change the subject.

'Well, let's not talk about that yet. Let's deal with one thing at a time,' said Mary as she glanced through her notes.

Bridgette nodded in silent agreement.

'I could take a look through the records to see if I can find an address for you. Then I could write, but it may not be easy. You do appreciate that when you were adopted, the mothers thought there was never going to be any chance their children would trace them. It's only with the change of law that it's possible. As I said, earlier, you should talk to a social worker before any meeting takes place.'

Bridgette thought for a while. What a lot of hassle, I thought it would be easier than this.

What if we write and she doesn't want any communication? That's something you'll have to face. It's a strong possibility. Quite a lot of parents don't want to know about their children after so many years. You can't force someone to get in contact if they don't want to. This can be upsetting for everyone.

Bridgette shuffled around in her seat. The chair was uncomfortable because the pad was gone, and she felt very emotional.

'In the meantime, Bridgette, I would strongly recommend that you come to a decision about your own baby because time goes very fast. I can't tell you what to do, but I can only say from experience, that giving up a baby is very traumatic and it's not always necessary nowadays when you can get financial help. Will your parents have you back?'

Bridgette thought for what seemed like hours before she said, 'I don't know.'

'Well, what I suggest is you go and have a think about things for a couple of days and then get in contact with me again. If you leave me your mother's details, I'll write a letter to her, and we will see if there is any response, but I'm not making any promises.'

Bridgette felt very strange inside because she'd never considered the possibility that her mother might not reply to a letter, but it made sense that she may not want her contact. For years, she'd visualised a reunion where they put their arms around each other and accepted each other back into their lives. Now suddenly, her childhood dreams were brought into reality. Was she ready to face this? Panic gripped her, and she began breathing rapidly. 'I thought things would be easier than this,' she whispered.

'I used to think like that, but when I lost my baby all those years ago, my whole life changed. Time goes so fast, and sometimes it's better not to know,' added Sister Mary.

'You lost a baby?' Bridgette cried out in alarm.

Sister Mary held the cross around her neck and lowered her head in prayer.

'Yes, I did, but it was a very long time ago, and even now, I'm not entirely sure. For years I was told my child was dead, but a few months ago, I found an unexpected letter, and it's possible that she was taken to America.'

Bridgette couldn't believe her ears; a pregnant nun. Did that happen? What sort of place was this? But with one look into Sister Mary's eyes, she completely understood. First, she was a mother and then she was a nun.

'I'm sorry,' Bridgette replied, and she genuinely meant it. Although it was shocking, she felt a strong feeling of empathy towards Mary. Were her emotions up and down due to her pregnancy, or discussing her adoption?

Bridgette had always considered herself lucky because she knew there were far worse places to be brought up. She could have suffered some terrible things in her life. As an adopted child, she'd enjoyed a great childhood, where she was loved. It was sad her parents had argued about her being a nanny, but they only wanted the best for her. She sat in silence for what seemed a very long time.

Mary bowed her head again for several moments in prayer, which Bridgette felt was the obvious thing to do. Bridgette prayed quietly asking for answers, but in her heart, she already knew. When Sister Mary finally looked up, she said, 'I've decided. I want to keep my baby, but I'd still like you to send a letter to my mother. Her name is Rebecca O'Brien. Here are all the details I have about her, plus my date of birth and current address.

'I understand,' replied Mary, who was surprised at herself for revealing the loss of her child to such a young girl but Bridgette appeared very mature for her age, and she certainly wasn't afraid of saying what she wanted. Perhaps she knew all along, and it was just a matter of her finding the strength? God always helped with that.

'You, said that you went home for a few weeks at the end of the summer. How can you be sure that Mark isn't the father?' asked Mary.

Mary was worried about upsetting the girl but she had to ask the question.

'No, the baby isn't Mark's child, if only things were that simple. Mark and I are over. There was an incident, but it was about a month before, and I'm sure of my dates,' replied Bridgette. She still felt guilty about the way she had treated Mark, but she didn't want to discuss it.

'Oh, I understand. It's difficult for you, but I feel that God will guide you to make the right decision. Goodbye Bridgette, we'll speak again soon, but please take your time and think carefully.'

As Bridgette turned to leave, Mary suddenly handed her a small bible.

'Please take this. It was mine when I was your age. Hopefully, you'll find some words in there that will bring you comfort. It was very special to me, so please look after it,' said Mary, in a whisper.

'Of course, I'll treasure it, thank you', replied Bridgette, as she put the bible in her handbag and started to button up her coat.

Bridgette quickly walked out of St. Catherine's, into the cold autumn air and breathed a huge sigh of relief. She was unsure if she would ever look at the bible, but she intended keeping it. Perhaps one day, it would bring her comfort.

At one time St. Catherine's may have been grand, but now it was shabby. It certainly wasn't a place that anyone would want to spend any time in, she thought, hastily walked away. Poor Rebecca, it must have been hard. Tears began to stream down Bridgette's face. It was impossible to hold them back any longer. She didn't know if she was crying for Rebecca, herself, or the baby or because history was repeating itself!

Bridgette looked at her watch, it was 3.15 pm. There would be another bus in about fifteen minutes. At least now, there was one decision less, she concluded as she sprang into step along the leafy path. For a few minutes, she felt almost happy, she was so relieved to have shared her burden. Sister Mary had understood because she'd been through it herself, although, Bridgette was still perplexed. How on earth did that happen?

CHAPTER 20
MARK

Mark felt a mixture of shock and anger that Bridgette was pregnant! Had she planned on keeping it a secret, or worse have an abortion without telling him. She'd carry on with her life without giving him a second thought and he was the father! He knew that she was settled in her new career, in Surrey, but how many friends knew about her pregnancy? Why hadn't she been in touch with him and why did he have to hear the news second hand from Jane? He'd assumed that Bridgette was happily working as a nanny because none of their friends had spoken about her for weeks until Jane rang. There hadn't been a word since she returned to Surrey at the end of the summer. Jane appeared to be the only friend she'd been in touch with. His friends were always asking if he'd heard from Bridgette and he was lost for words. It had become embarrassing.

Mark didn't understand why they broke up. He initially thought he was going to visit her at the weekends, but it hadn't been like that because she hadn't bothered to reply to his letters. What happened between them after her 18th birthday celebration, had made things worse, but he still hoped they'd reconcile. Mark's heart ached. Although this wasn't something, he'd readily admit, he knew he was in love with her. Despite this, it inexcusable that she hadn't contacted him about the pregnancy.

Mark thought about Bridgette most of the time. He couldn't get the image of her out of his head, particularly the day she told him she planned to be a nanny because she was bored with everything and needed a challenge. He wasn't sure if her 'bored of everything', included him, but it dawned on him over the following weeks that it did. After that, he began to see a lot less of her until the relationship dwindled. Bridgette was so friendly when they were together in the summer, it was as if they'd recovered their old passion. He couldn't understand how she could be like that one minute and the next she didn't want to know. Why couldn't she see what they had? He'd do anything to give her the life she wanted. He appreciated they were both young but he had hoped at some point, they'd become engaged and eventually marry.

As time went on, Mark realised the pain of losing Bridgette had started to fade. He'd resolved that he'd soon meet someone new but he still doubted any relationship would have the same connection. So, when the phone rang at half-past seven, and it was Jane, Bridgette's oldest friend, he was shocked. He assumed that she was worried about her lack of contact, but he was wrong! Unfortunately, at the mention of her name his feelings quickly surfaced, and he began probing Jane about their mysterious weekend in London. He realised that he still wanted to see her if only to talk about what had happened that night down by the river. However, he was totally unprepared for Jane's news about the pregnancy.

The first thing he wanted to ask was how many weeks was she? How could he be sure the baby was his? He hastily looked in his diary as he tried to remember the date of their get together after the William. It was a definite possibility, but him a father? There was a feeling of unreality about it. It must have been early September at the end of the summer? They'd both had too much to drink, and then there was the fantastic sex in his car. At least he thought so. He was unlikely to forget what happened between them, but he certainly didn't remember the actual date. He'd thought at the time that they'd get back together, but it soon became evident that Bridgette was keeping her distance. Mark felt as if she wasn't even there, did she have someone else on her mind? If they hadn't got drunk, he knew that it would never have happened. He was annoyed with Bridgette for messing around with his feelings. He hadn't told anyone what happened that night because he felt used. Why did she encourage him to do it? She was the one who started kissing him when he'd planned on taking her home.

Jane declared he was the father of the baby. He hadn't wanted to believe it at first, but when she explained that Bridgette hadn't been anywhere on her own, because she worked such long hours, he started to believe it must be true. How could Bridgette have met someone in the short time she'd been living in Surrey? The more Mark thought about it, the more convinced he became. Although he was shocked. He secretly also pleased.

Mark sat down to drink his cup of tea and began to flick through the television channels looking for football. He enjoyed football, and he'd see a live match occasionally, but it was expensive. He wanted to phone Bridgette but what would he say? She might reject him for a second time. What if he he'd got this wrong? If he asked Jane for her address, he could just turn. Perhaps it was better to face the situation head-on, then at least he'd discover the truth!

CHAPTER 21
REBECCA IN SCOTLAND

Rebecca was perched on a large rock, in one of the most beautiful places she'd ever experienced. Lawrence had gone for a walk. They both loved walking, but he wanted to climb further than she could manage. So, he took his binoculars and strode on ahead. Lawrence enjoyed walking on his own, searching for birds of prey and he also enjoyed painting them. They'd parked the car by the banks of the river Dee. Rebecca was happy to wait in the car with her book, a flask of hot soup and a blanket while Lawrence walked the few extra miles, because it was freezing. He said he wouldn't be too long because they wanted to be back at the cottage before dark which appeared to happen very quickly.

The surrounding scenery was so stunning that Rebecca soon put her book down. She left the car and began to walk up a gentle slope. There was a large rock, which made an excellent place to sit and contemplate. The sound of the fast-flowing river soothed her, as the water melodiously hit the stones. The trees swayed and creaked in the breeze, and there were various bird songs that she couldn't easily recognise. Lawrence knew the names of many birds. He was knowledgeable about wildlife, but Rebecca only knew a few.

The Dee, Rebecca had been told, was the famous Scottish river, where the royal children were taught to fish. She could see the occasional salmon jumping to the surface as it raced against the current. They were right on the edge of the Cairngorm Mountains.

They must have been mad deciding on Scotland, in December, thought Rebecca as she rubbed her hands together to keep warm, but it was the only time they could both take a holiday off work. It was now only a week until Christmas and Lawrence wanted them to spend some time where he intended to buy a house in his retirement. They'd taken the cottage for two weeks, and they planned to stay until the New Year. Yesterday, they'd shopped in Aberdeen which was sometimes known as granite city. Rebecca had never seen such a grim-looking place, but it was winter and the days were short. She thought London was bleak at times, but it was lively in comparison to this grey monstrosity. The looming buildings were soulless, and she was glad when they left and took to the country roads to find the cottage. The roads were windy, narrow and extraordinarily steep. Scotland appeared vast, with little signs of civilisation for miles. There were endless trees in their beautiful winter colours, which took her breath away. Rebecca had a feeling of inner peace, and she was not hardly surprised that Lawrence wanted to relocate here. Scotland had many rivers, hills and trees, yet, it felt lonely. She sighed and looked up to a line of trees on the horizon. She could just make out Lawrence in the distance. She hoped that he'd taken some good shots of eagles because she didn't want to hang around for much longer in this temperature. It was icy!

Rebecca felt in her pocket for the folded-up piece of paper. She hadn't had much time to digest the information in London because the letter arrived as she was frantically packing. She very carefully unfolded it with her gloves on, which was no easy task, and read it once again.

Dear Rebecca,

One of your old friends has contacted me to ask me to get in touch with you because she doesn't know your address. I believe you knew her well in 1962, her name is Bridgette, and she's planning a school reunion. You may well remember her? I'm sure she'll be delighted if you can get in touch. I've left my phone number at the bottom of this letter and eagerly await your response.

With kind regards,
Mary

The address on the top didn't say St Catherine's but Rebecca immediately recognised the rest of the address. She guessed that the letter was written this way in case it fell into the wrong hands. She quickly folded the correspondence and placed it back in her pocket. Tears began to roll down her face as she hastily searched for a tissue in her handbag. Lawrence mustn't see her like this because if he found out, he could reject her. What on earth would he make of it? She didn't want to risk, the best thing that had happened to her, for someone she didn't know! How could this be her Bridgette when in her mind, her child was still a baby. Her Bridgette was meant to be happy and loved by two people. What on earth did she want after all these years? How could she be expected to explain to her child that many years ago, she'd been a foolish young girl!

Rebecca followed the path back to the car and opened the door. It was Lawrence's car, but they shared the driving. She started the engine and tried to get some warm air blowing to defrost her frozen face and melt away her tears. It must be minus five out there, she thought. Lawrence must be mad going for such a long walk when it's this cold, and it will be dark soon. Just as Rebecca thought about the craziness of the situation, a cheerful Lawrence appeared.

'I walked right around in a loop. It wasn't that far. I've got some great pictures to show you. Guess what, I also found an osprey nest. It's absolutely amazing up there. I'll have to go back,' Lawrence said, like an excited schoolboy.

They drove back to the cottage and quickly started a roaring log fire. It wouldn't be long before it was bed time. It was an enjoyable holiday and a much-needed break from London, but it certainly wasn't what everyone would choose, thought Rebecca as she moved closer to the fire.

The next morning, Rebecca snuggled up next to Lawrence, under the covers of their warm bed. He was still sleeping peacefully, so she looked across at the alarm clock resting on the bedside table. She noticed it was almost eight o'clock. The cottage they'd rented in Deeside was proving to be very cosy. It had a small inglenook fireplace, plenty of logs, and electric radiators in each of the bedrooms. The owner rented it for most of the year, but it was easier to book in the winter and it was cheaper. It had been decorated with extremely tasteful wallpaper, and every effort had been made with the furnishings. The sturdy pine table, chairs, beds, and wardrobes all matched. There were deep pile carpets throughout which gave the cottage a feeling of real comfort, and the bathroom had cork tiles which extended up the side of a white bath. There was a double room, a twin-bedded room and a single room. Rebecca thought it a shame they were only occupying one bedroom. Perhaps if things worked out well, they could bring some friends in the summer.

Rebecca walked down the stairs and opened the kitchen door, trying to be as quiet as possible so as not to disturb Lawrence. Rebecca found the kettle and made a cup of tea, and a few minutes later, she gazed in awe at the view out of the window which overlooked the nearby cairngorms. She reached for her handbag and she once again read the letter from Sister Mary. As she read, a lump started to develop in her throat, and a slight pain in her chest. The correspondence had a suffocating effect on her. It made her feel so emotional, and she didn't know if she would ever be able to deal with these feelings. Her thoughts immediately took her to the cold lonely flat and the strong smell of tobacco from the cigarette factory.

I can't get in touch with her, it's just too painful. Not now, not, after all this time. Somewhere inside, though, Rebecca knew she wanted to see little Bridgette again, but it was hard to associate the eighteen-year-old girl with the baby she left. She also wondered about Lawrence. How would he react? She had managed to keep this to herself, for so many years. It was also possible that Bridgette would want to know about her father, which was another tricky thing. Rebecca shuddered at the thought. That was somewhere she didn't want to venture! All the painful feelings had begun to surface along with the emotions.

The kettle boiled and Rebecca made just one cup of tea. She decided to take Lawrence one when he awoke because she didn't want to disturb him after all that driving. He must be exhausted. I'll have to phone Mary and tell her I'm sorry, but I can't meet Bridgette, or whatever her name is now, because it's just too difficult for me. The girl will get over it. She has her parents, and all I have is Lawrence. I can't risk ruining the relationships I've spent my life building, after all, I gave her up so she'd have a good home with parents who'd love her, so I don't owe her anything.

'Oh God, why did this have to happen?' she said aloud.

Rebecca suddenly heard movement from upstairs, and put the kettle back on to make sure that Lawrence's tea was hot. This cooker can't be too difficult, she mumbled. It was electric, and there was a gas cooker at the flat, so the temperature dials were different. She had offered to make Lawrence bacon and eggs that morning because they were going to visit Balmoral Castle. She wondered if the Queen was already home for Christmas. Perhaps her flags would be flying.

Rebecca decided that it would be easier not to mention Bridgette to Lawrence. There was no need now and he wouldn't find the letter. The situation made her feel a little guilty and uncomfortable but she'd never been her mother. A birth mother, was an entirely different relationship. What did the girl expect?

The following week the telephone rang in Sister Mary's office, which surprised her because she was still winding down and things had turned quiet.

'Hello, Sister Mary' answered the sister in a friendly and efficient voice. There was definitely a note of happiness in her voice today because the day had finally arrived when She officially left St. Catherine's to start her new role in the community, and she was absolutely thrilled. Mary couldn't wait to pass her duties over to Sister Evelyn, who was taking over her position for a few months. Sister Evelyn had been Mary's assistant for many years and she enjoyed her work. Mary knew the nun would make an excellent replacement because she was very capable.

'Hello is that, Mary?' asked Rebecca in the voice that she usually saved for work.

'Yes, who is that please?'

'It's Rebecca, you wrote to me last week about getting in contact with you. Bridgette wants to get in touch with me?'

'Yes, that's right, she does. She came to see me last week, and she'd love to know a little more about you. I know how difficult it must be for you after all these years. It's probably a huge shock, but your daughter has wanted to contact you, for several years. She'll be delighted that we've found you.'

Rebecca was silent for several moments. It made her feel sad, but it wasn't the right time to meet.

'I know this sounds really mean and not what Bridgette will want to hear, but it's impossible to meet her at the moment. I'm not saying that I'll never have contact with her, but it would cause me too much stress. I've been through some difficult times, and things have been a struggle. My partner doesn't know about Bridgette, so I can't run the risk of him finding out,' explained Rebecca. Her voice was wavering quite a lot because the contact with the sister was almost too much to bear. She did remember Sister Mary, vaguely, for being one of the kinder nuns, but she wasn't ready to talk to anyone about the past.

Sister Mary sighed deeply. This wasn't good news, especially hearing it today when things had started so well! It would be particularly hard for Bridgette because the girl had her own problems, but Mary could also understand Rebecca's reaction. She'd given Bridgette up eighteen years ago, and she had been forced to move on. It would have been harrowing for her, and she didn't want to revisit it. Sister Mary quickly realised how easy it was for her to become involved. Over the years, she'd always wanted the best for the girls, and at times her involvement had turned into a problem because she felt the girls' pain and here it was again, another let-down, another person to disappoint. Life could be cruel.

'Are you sure?' she replied, giving Rebecca a few moments to reconsider.

'Yes, I'm sure. I can't see Bridget because my life has so many ups and downs and I'm finding it hard to cope. Maybe one day, when it feels the right time, I'll get in touch. I'm sure you understand. You must have come across other parents in this situation.'

Although Mary knew precisely how Rebecca felt, it was still disappointing, and she felt for the girl, especially in her condition. Her instinct was to tell Rebecca that Bridgette was pregnant, but Mary realised it would only complicate matters. It was also manipulative.

'Well, it's a pity, but I understand. Please don't hesitate to get in touch with us in the future, if we can be of any help, Rebecca,' said Mary, returning to her official voice. Sister Mary replaced the telephone receiver and then started her last duty of the day, writing letters. She decided to write to Bridgette immediately so she could put it behind her. She didn't want to think any more about it and she was relieved that her job was coming to an end. In a strange kind of way, her life had just begun!

CHAPTER 22
SAYING GOODBYE

It was seven o'clock, and Bridgette's alarm clock was buzzing. It was now only ten days until Christmas, and she was working until the end of the week then returning home. She dragged herself out of bed and noticed that her morning sickness had practically gone! This was a massive relief as it made it easier to take the children to school. This morning, Carmel was also going to nursery, which meant Bridgette could come back and have some peace for a couple of hours. The children were full of Christmas songs, decorations and why Daddy hadn't got them a Christmas tree! Neil assured them that their tree would definitely be up this weekend. They were going to have a real tree this year and they'd decorate it together on Sunday.

Bridgette felt sad. She wanted to go home for Christmas but she'd miss some special moments with the children. Bridgette loved Christmas, and so far, everything had been terrific fun. Far more fun than when she was a child! It had been months since she saw her family and they were excited about her coming back. She missed her parents and Fiona, and they needed to catch up. She'd have to break the news sometime over Christmas and that she intended keeping the baby. It would no doubt be a shock to them. She also planned to tell Neil before she left, but finding the opportunity was difficult because he was seldom on his own. Bridgette wanted to stay to be close to him, even if it was unrealistic. When she looked at Neil, she couldn't imagine being away. The thought of never seeing him again was unbearable. She regularly told herself that he wasn't hers to have. Living with the family meant she could see him as much as she liked, although they couldn't be intimate. Neil had appeared very moody and withdrawn over the past few days. She got the impression things weren't going well with Karen. Perhaps he'll leave her, and we can get somewhere together, thought Bridgette naively, but part of her already knew that was impossible. How on earth would the children react? It would be too confusing. Although she'd formed a close bond with them, she wasn't their mother, and how could Daddy be with their nanny!

Bridgette quickly got dressed and came downstairs to the kitchen. It looked as if Karen and Neil had already had their breakfast and gone to work. It was half-past seven, and they often left early because Neil had to check in with his insurance office once a week in the city. Karen always left early. She was an early riser. The older two were already dressed, and Jonathan had turned on the television to watch cartoons, while Lucy was sitting at the kitchen table going over yesterday's homework. Carmel was playing with some Lego in front of the TV. She was still in her pyjamas.

'Come on you lot, it's time for breakfast. We'd better hurry up, or we'll be late,' said Bridgette.

It seemed like no time at all until she'd packed the children with their school bags, into the car and headed off. Thank goodness Carmel was at the nursery today, two whole hours to herself! What on earth would she do? But she knew by the time all the breakfast things were washed, and the housework finished, there would only be about an hour left. Without having any friends in the area, she'd probably end up watching television and drinking tea. Then it would be time to collect Carmel because the mornings went by like a flash!

Bridgette hadn't long been back from the school run and was watching breakfast television when there was a firm knock at the front door. She got up from the sofa and wondered where her purse was. It was probably a charity this time in the morning, and it was quicker to use her money than to look for any that Karen and Neil had left around. As she approached the front door, she saw the outline of a tall man through the glass. For a minute, Bridgette thought she recognised the height and stance of the person, and she walked towards the front door to open it.

'Mark, what on earth are you doing here?' she gasped.

'Bridgette' he replied, leaning towards her to give her a kiss. It's so good to see you. I've got the day off today, so I thought I'd come and see how you're doing,' he replied, enthusiastically.

To her surprise, Bridgette was genuinely pleased to see him, and she leaned forward to kiss him on the cheek.

'Come in. I'm only watching the television at the moment until it's time for me to collect Carmel from the nursery. Carmel is the little girl I look after. Well, one of the children. There are two more.'

'Three children!' said Mark, who was genuinely surprised.

'Yes, three, I'm always busy, never stop. I didn't know looking after kids would be such hard work!' She heaved a sigh and started to walk out of the hallway towards the kitchen at the end of the corridor.

'Would you like a cup of tea Mark, toast, or something?'

'Yes, thanks. That'll be great. I had to get an early train from Suffolk then the tube, it's great to see you Bridgette, but you look tired. Jane has been anxious about you; she says she hasn't heard from you much. No-one has, none of the old crowd we used to go out with, in Ipswich. Anyway, I want all your news, and I understand that I'm soon to be a father!'

Bridgette suddenly dropped the empty mug she was holding, which shattered into pieces. Bits of crockery flew out in various directions all over the kitchen floor. Her heart seemed to stop right there because she couldn't believe what Mark had just said. She tried to express herself, but she was stuck for words.

'How on earth did you? Oh, it must have been Jane,' she finally squeaked.

'Well actually it was, but I don't want you to be cross, Bridgette, because Jane has been really concerned about you. Although I was really shocked at the time, I'm sort of getting used to the idea now.

Bridgette started to sweep up the crockery from the kitchen floor and wondered what to say to Mark. It crossed her mind to tell him the truth, that her baby was Neil's, but if she told him the real story, she would have to cope with everything on her own. If her parents knew Neil was the father, they would go mad, and she wouldn't be accepted home. But if Mark were the father, it wouldn't be such a problem. Mark had caught her completely unaware because she wanted to tell Neil about the baby first. Her heart kept saying, I really like Mark, but I love Neil. Life is so complicated, or was she perhaps plain unlucky? Here was a man who wanted her and she wanted someone who didn't care about her. They were both very young, and things may be a little awkward at first, but at least if she was with Mark, she could keep her baby. He would support her.

'I'll make us some toast, while you make the tea, Bridgette. Show me where the bread's kept?' Mark insisted. Bridgette pointed in the direction of the bread bin and made the tea.

'Mark, I've missed you. I'm really sorry I didn't tell you about the baby straight away, but I was worried about how you would react, especially as I was so mean to you. I said some pretty horrible things about how my life was boring and other things before I left. I didn't know if you'd still want to know me, especially after what happened in the summer. I should never have done that to you. It wasn't fair, I'm sorry.'

Mark took the tea and the toast he'd made over to the little pine table. The table that reminded Bridgette of Neil. Every morning while the children ate their breakfast, she relived what happened between them that evening. Bridgette sat down next to Mark and realised that she did feel comfortable with him, but there was no excitement. Would it be enough when her feelings might never develop into nothing more than friendship?

Mark sat on the same side of the table as Bridgette and turned slightly on his seat to face her. He looked into her eyes for ages. Then said, 'Bridgette, I hope that I don't make a right idiot of myself by saying this, but since you left, I realise I love you. I should never have let you go. I'm sorry that you got bored. Perhaps I didn't make enough effort to listen to you. I should have taken you out to more places and done more with you. It was hardly surprising that you wanted to move on. Anyway, I'm here now, aren't I? Surely that shows you that I want us to be together with the baby.'

Bridgette found it very hard to look Mark in the eyes. His honesty was unnerving, and she didn't want him to discover her true feelings because she was fond of him. She had hurt him once and doing it again was unfair but it seemed her only choice.

'Let's give it another go then. I'm leaving here at the end of the week, and I'm not sure it's worth me coming back. I'll have to talk to Mum and Dad because I haven't told them yet. I hope that not too many people know about this. Perhaps you can come with me to talk to my parents, and we'll face them together?' Bridgette realised she was making a life-changing decision and hoped that Mark would stick by her.

'I'd be pleased to,' Mark replied' as he gripped her hand in reassurance.

CHAPTER 23
GOING HOME

It was Saturday and Karen, and Neil were at home together for once! There were so many domestic chores to be finished, plus a Christmas tree had arrived! However, clean the house was, it would soon become untidy with three small children. Carmel was excited today; she was jumping up and down shouting 'the Christmas tree,' giving everyone a bit of a headache, and it was only ten o'clock in the morning! Bridgette kissed the girls' goodbye and ruffled Jonathan's hair. Kisses had become embarrassing, and she didn't want him to feel awkward in front of his parents.

Bridgette was packed and ready to go. Her suitcase stood in the hallway while she waited for Neil to get out his car. He decided to take her all the way to Liverpool Street station, the same as he had done in the summer. This was a crazy idea because it was Christmas and it would take hours, but Neil was adamant about it. He wanted to make sure Bridgette was well looked after on her last day with them.

The children were hoping for a white Christmas, but as Bridgette didn't enjoy the snow, she hoped it would stay as it was now, bright but cold. Bridgette told Karen and Neil that she'd be back in January, at the end of the Christmas holidays. Fortunately, they both had two weeks leave so they could spend Christmas together, and Grandma was coming as well. This time of year, was a quiet time at work for both of them, so that made things easier. With hugs and kisses done, Neil put Bridgette's suitcase in the boot of his car.

The BMW was out today because Neil didn't use the MG in the winter, because, with all the salt on the roads, it could rust. Bridgette got in and immediately felt the comfort of the warm car. It had all the trimmings, electric windows, a blue-tinted glass windscreen, places to put a drink, an inbuilt stereo and heated seats. It was a real home from home! She suddenly felt sad because it was likely the last time she'd see Neil, and he appeared to be in a quiet, reflective mood. She'd wanted to tell him about the baby but it was impossible because over the last few weeks, he was never alone. Perhaps he'd withdrawn because he had problems at work or with Karen? Anyway, her decision was made about leaving, so she had to stick to it, even if it hurt.

Neil turned on the radio and tuned it to a jazz station which Bridgette felt was for her benefit. She relaxed and for a short time she closed her eyes. She imagined herself back with Neil in the bedroom where they had spent the night together only a few weeks ago. Neil's hand left the steering wheel and touched her hand as if he were reading her thoughts.

'I'll miss you Bridgette,' he said.

'Don't be silly, of course you won't. It's Christmas, and there are loads of things to do with Karen and the kids. You'll have a great time together.' I will miss you too, Bridgette whispered silently under her breath, but the sound of her whisper was quickly lost amongst the music and the gentle hum of the car. She suddenly felt tired and started to drift in and out of sleep. It was impossible to return because Neil had broken her heart, and there was no choice but to look forward to her future. Her new life awaited her, an experience that would be very different with Mark and the baby.

CHAPTER 24
JANUARY

Neil kicked the side of the living room door. He was angry. It was more out of frustration than anything else, but it made the children jump.

'Do you have to do that, Neil? I know you're annoyed at taking the children to school but what else can we do until we find a replacement? Bridgette was so good. It's hard finding anyone the children like!' shouted Karen.

'You would think she'd have at least phoned to say she wasn't coming back! But no, we're left in the lurch with an explanation. Did she give you any indication she was leaving? I don't know what goes on in these young peoples' heads. They only think about themselves,' shouted Neil.

Neil couldn't express how he really felt, to Karen, but he had his suspicions, why she hadn't been in touch. His mind wandered back to the times she felt unwell but it was too late to think about it now. What difference would it make? One pregnant Nanny had already left, and if Karen found out Bridgette was expecting, their marriage would be over. Not that it was worth saving when Karen was so selfish! She didn't appear to care about the children. It was all work and meetings and God knows what else!

Karen slammed the front door. She was also angry. Why did Neil have to complain about everything? Surely it wasn't that hard to run the children to school when he worked at home, but he seemed insistent on making her life difficult. He knew how demanding her job was. It was only in the interim because they'd have a new nanny soon. Neil could be such a baby. When she married him, it was fun being with a younger man, but that was then. Things had changed, and she didn't want to spend hardly any time with him unless it was absolutely necessary because of the children. Bridgette was the second Nanny who had left. Wasn't that a little odd? When her friends suggested that Neil may have had something to do with it, she had laughed, but it was very suspicious. She wasn't entirely sure. It was feasible that Neil may have upset her in some way or worse? How did she know what Neil got up to when he hardly communicated?

Neil picked up the post from the doormat, which Karen had left in her urgency to leave for work. Amongst the usual recognisable pile of bills, Neil was surprised to find a letter addressed to Bridgette. He was curious that someone would write to her at this address. What on earth was the girl up to? Perhaps she'd applied for job and hadn't told them. That could account for why she left without a word. Neil felt extremely agitated by the letter, and he was annoyed at himself for letting a young girl affect him so strongly. He was sure some of his anger was due to feelings he had for her, but he was furious at her for leaving them in the lurch. Before considering it any further, Neil ripped the letter in half and chucked it in the kitchen bin. Whatever it was about, he wasn't sending it on. Tough luck, Bridgette. He wasn't going to give her anything, not even a reference unless she got in touch with them and explained what was going on! I hope she had a damned good reason for disappearing because this is inexcusable. It may be difficult to replace her but surely, there were other good nannies out there? But in Neil's heart, he doubted it. He knew Bridgette had been brilliant with the children and now she'd gone. He also knew that most of his frustration was because he'd behaved like an idiot. It's my fault, he thought, as he drove the children to school. A man of my age should have known better than to seduce an eighteen-year-old girl. Did he ever learn!

CHAPTER 25
SEVEN MONTHS LATER

It was nearly August, and the weather was scorching. The outside temperature was ninety degrees, and it wasn't the best day to give birth to a child. The hospital fans were going full pelt, and the windows were wide open. Bridgette was sweltering. She had been admitted to Ipswich hospital in the early hours of the morning after her waters had broken. It was now two in the afternoon, and things had started to happen.

'Push, push' screamed the nurse who held her hand for Bridgette to squeeze. A young trainee doctor stood at the other side of her, and they were both encouraging her to keep going. Mark was waiting eagerly at the foot of the bed, looking for the baby's head.

'I can see it,' he shouted excitedly.

Okay, keep pushing Bridgette. Don't give up now, you're nearly there,' said the young Doctor. Bridgette needed all of her strength to push, and she didn't really care whether anyone could see the head, or not, as long as this baby came out soon. It felt enormous. It couldn't possibly leave her body.

Giving birth to something this big was a physical impossibility. Sweat ran off her, soaking where she lay. She'd never expected to feel pain like this nor was she told that the contractions could be so close together. One final shove she thought, hoping that her weak muscles could muster up a last bit of strength.

'That's it, well done Bridgette, that's the head out,' they shouted. Then the rest of the body emerged quickly. At last, her struggle was over and just as well, as an exhausted Bridgette had no more pushes to give. Not one ounce of energy was left in her weak body. How on earth did people do this and go for it a second time? It certainly wasn't how it looked in films or childbirth classes.

The nurse picked up the baby, who was surprisingly quite clean and wrapped the child in a thick sheet, then handed the baby to Bridgette.

'What is it?' she asked in a weak voice.

'He's a boy' replied the nurse.

Wow, I've produced a boy. Mark wanted a boy, she thought and smiled.

'He weighs eight and a half pounds. A very healthy weight for a first,' said the nurse. 'What are you going to call him?''

'William George,' stated Bridgette confidently.

'William never knew he was a father,' Bridgette whispered. Sometime later, when she'd returned to the ward, William had been put into a large plastic cot next to her bed. He was sleeping peacefully, and he looked very healthy with plenty of colour. He didn't have jaundice like some of the babies. She'd also been able to feed him a little. Bridgette smiled to herself. She was amazed at what she'd accomplished. A real human being! It seemed absolutely incredible, almost impossible. She put her little finger to his hand, and he opened his tiny fist and gripped it. He couldn't open his eyes yet, it was too early, perhaps tomorrow.

William was a work of art. He was perfect, and he made her feel special. Finally, there was someone in the world who looked like her. From now on, she wouldn't be alone in a world of photographs where other people matched and she never did. They would be a matching pair, mother and son with perhaps some of the same features, which she'd love. William made her feel special, and there was so much to look forward to.

Mark came in through the door and walked over to look at the baby.

'Isn't he great? He really looks like you.'

'I want all of our children to look like me,' said Bridgette a little selfishly. Mark just laughed.

'He'll play for Ipswich Town when he grows up. I can see those footballers' knees already.'

'Yes, well, he's not just like me,' said Bridgette, with a slight laugh but her stomach was still very sore from the birth.

'I'll let you get some rest and come and see you later,' said Mark beaming. It wasn't long before Bridgette and William were asleep.

CHAPTER 26
ONE YEAR LATER

Today was William's first birthday. Mark and Bridgette were very excited. They'd managed to find a flat not far from Mark's parents, and they visited them frequently. Her parents were coming for tea today and Mark's mum was coming with a birthday cake with just one candle for William blow out. Bridgette's parents hadn't taken the news of her pregnancy well. Fortunately, time was a great healer, and now one year later, they'd grown used to Bridgette being a mother. She was a good mother, and they were proud of her. After all, they were pleased she could have children and they were now grandparents. They'd soon slipped into the role without any criticism of either Bridgette or Mark.

It was also apparent to them that Mark was a great dad. He'd made their little flat really lovely, and he'd also worked on William's room for hours. He wanted to get everything just right, for their little boy. Despite the flat only having two bedrooms, there was plenty of room for the three of them. They were also close to a local park, which gave Bridgette somewhere to walk with William while Mark was at work.

Mark now worked as a graphic designer for a local, independent travel company which was rapidly moving forward in a competitive market. Mark loved his job. Although he had to bring some of his projects, home, William's playtime was never compromised. Mark showed him how to chalk on a small blackboard, stack bricks and he frequently read him stories. He even changed his nappy without being asked!

Bridgette was happy although she sometimes missed the children she'd worked with, especially Carmel but William was beautiful. He was everything she wanted, and her life was full and busy. She was happy the way her parents had taken to Mark. They'd made him one of the family by respecting his wishes and opinions. They recognised he had a real talent for art and graphics and her father was interested in his work. Bridgette couldn't believe that William was one. Time had gone so quickly. She was also surprised at the number of birthday cards he'd received today; no-one had forgotten him.

Mark had taken William out for a walk to the local park. He's been gone a long time, thought Bridgette. He's probably got William in one of those new baby swings, she thought. They'll be having great fun. Bridgette was meant to make sandwiches and prepare the jelly for her parents' arrival at four, but she'd spent most of the time clearing up and re-arranging the flat. The trouble was it could get really messy with all the things they needed for William. They just seemed to accumulate more stuff! She suddenly noticed that at the bottom of the pile of birthday cards, there was a letter addressed to her. It looked as if it had been re-directed from London. Had her mail finally been re-directed? When she noticed that some of her regular mail wasn't turning up at the flat, she realised something must have been happening to it. Whatever the reason, it was annoying! She didn't recognise the handwriting on the envelope, but it appeared personal, so she carefully opened the envelope and unfolded the letter.

Dearest Bridgette,

I'm sorry that I took so long to respond to your request to meet, but when you first contacted me, I couldn't cope with our contact. My partner, Lawrence, knows nothing of your existence, and I didn't want to lie to him but I've now decided that if I meet you, I will tell Lawrence everything. At present, he's filming in the States for a month, so it would be a good time to meet. As I've taken so long to respond to you, I'm wondering whether you still want to do this? I didn't explain myself very well to Sister Mary, who should have let you know what was going on. It was never my intention not to meet you, I just needed more time.

My phone number is at the top of this letter if you want to telephone me.

Yours truly,
Rebecca O'Brien

Bridgette reread the letter. She'd given up all hope of meeting Rebecca, and now Rebecca wanted to meet her when she had got used to the idea they may never meet. This had come like a bolt, out of the blue. Bridgette didn't know if she could cope with hearing why her mother hadn't kept her. She was prepared to listen to the truth before she had William but now things were different. Feelings of rejection could re-surface and cause her to feel bad about herself when she wanted to be happy for William. She couldn't cope with confusion. What if Rebecca didn't like her? Or if she grew too fond of her, would she be able to have the same relationship with her parents? What sort of effect would this have on her happy family? Whatever happened from this point on, she knew that her relationship with Mark and William would never change. William was definitely her mum and dad's grandchild. He was their first grandchild, and they had earned the right to her love by looking after her for all those years. It also gave them the right to say Grandma and Granddad to William. This woman who she had wanted to meet for so many years, her birth mother, had suddenly become an unknown quantity. Bridgette knew that she'd now have to tell Rebecca who she could be in her life! It couldn't be the other way around because she already had so much love from the people around her. Her family were too important to upset.

Bridgette suddenly remembered the sandwiches and jelly. I'll telephone her tonight, she thought, when William's in bed. I'll also need time to explain to Mark, what's going on!

Mark was brilliant at the party. He was the perfect host. He made sure that everyone had something to eat and William was the centre of attention! He even took a few photographs of him in his high chair and helped him to blow out his single candle. Bridgette held the cake near him and blew as well, making the flame flicker before it went out. Everyone clapped at William's efforts. Bridgette was so proud of him. It was hard to imagine how anyone could give away a baby whatever the circumstances. Bridgette wondered if she'd even like Rebecca, which had never crossed her mind before. There was only one way to find out for sure, she'd have to go ahead and meet her.

When all the parents finally left at eight pm, Bridgette tucked up William in his cot, and for once, he looked as if he was dropping straight to sleep. He just lay there, with his eyes open for a few minutes, blinked and finally gave in. It had been a busy day. Mark said that when William was settled, he wanted to talk to her about something. Bridgette was full of curiosity. It wasn't often that Mark said things like that, unless he was serious. He was generally relaxed about everything and took challenges in his stride.

They sat in the living room, on their cottage style sofa, which was brought from a local second-hand shop. It was very comfortable if a little antiquated. It didn't go with the modern flat, but as there was only one salary now, they certainly couldn't afford to be fussy.

Mark looked very seriously at Bridgette and then quietly said, 'Bridgette, you know I love William, but sometimes I can't help wondering if he'll grow up realising that I'm not his real father. I wonder how he'll feel about that?'

Mark was full of surprises. She'd never once let on to him that he wasn't William's father. What was going on? There was no way he could have found out.

'You know, but, how could you?' she exclaimed.

'I think I've known all along. I guess I wanted to have a reason to look after you. When I thought back to the dates, I knew there was something not right. In the beginning, I thought you must have met someone else or had a fling while you were a nanny. As time went on, when you talked about Neil, I realised that something must have happened between you. I didn't want to believe it because the thought of you and Neil made me angry, but I now see that it's all in the past. When William was born, he was great, and I knew that I wanted to be with both of you. I decided it would be easier not to bring it up when we were all so happy.'

Bridgette suddenly realised that Mark had known far more than he he'd ever let on and she was shocked! In a way, she had taken him for a fool because she'd been unaware of how intuitive he was!

'I'm really sorry to have lied to you, Mark,' said Bridgette, with tears rolling down her face.

'I know pretending was the pits, but what else could I do? I really wanted to keep William, and I was scared that someone could try and take him away from me. I do love you, Mark, and you're a great father.'

'I'm a good father?' questioned Mark.

'Absolutely, the parents of the child, are the ones who do the looking after, they don't have to be the biological parent. A child's needs are love and attention, and we give William loads of that.'

'You did well today,' he said. 'Your mum and dad were really impressed,' he said, giving Bridgette a little squeeze.

'Thanks, Mark. I think we've both done well. William's a one-year-old! I can't believe that our baby has just had his first birthday.'

'Is he settled?' Mark asked, smiling at her.

'Yes, he's sound,' replied Bridgette, smiling back.

'Then shall we go up too?' he asked.

Bridgette responded by giving Mark a kiss on the lips. She seldom thought of Neil now, and she certainly didn't compare them. Mark was different. He was stable and reliable. That's all she wanted right now. Goodbye roller coaster, or was it goodbye? She took the piece of paper out of the envelope and put it carefully on the table. She'd phone Rebecca tomorrow, but for now, there was far more important business to attend to. It was time for her and Mark.

* * * * * * * * *

Bridgette constantly thought about the letter but she didn't phone Rebecca immediately. In fact, she felt quite nervous about the situation and wondered if she was doing the right thing. She finally plucked up the courage to telephone one Saturday morning, a few weeks later because Mark took William to see his parents. She knew he'd be gone for the rest of the day. Mark's parents adored William. His grandmother would play with him for hours.

Bridgette's fingers trembled as she dialled the telephone number in the letter. The telephone rang and rang. She was at the point of giving up and replacing the receiver, when a voice suddenly said, 'Hello.'

'Is that Rebecca?'

'Yes, is that Bridgette?'

'Yes,' she replied in a hushed and tentative voice. What had she let herself in for?

'I'm so pleased you rang. It must have been tough for you. You don't sound at all like I imagined. Look, there's so much to say to each other. We can't possibly say all the things we want to on the phone. I think the best thing is, you tell me when you have a free day and I come and visit you in Suffolk. Would that be all right?'

Bridgette thought for a moment. Of course, it would be all right! She'd been waiting for this day most of her life, but now that it was actually drawing near, she felt panicky. There were a lot of days they could meet, but their day had to be unique. It seemed as if there weren't enough time to arrange everything. What would she do with William, if Mark was at work? Who would look after him? Then, there was telling Mum and Dad about the meeting and how would they be about it? Suddenly Bridgette felt as if everything was happening far too quickly and she couldn't keep up.

When Rebecca said, 'Let's meet next week, at the local railway station,' Bridgette almost said, no. She was emotionally unprepared. Perhaps it would have been wiser to have seen a social worker first, as Sister Mary had suggested. Eventually she agreed to meet Rebecca on Tuesday. She'd make her lunch, although it would be an enormous challenge because it suddenly dawned on her that as she didn't know anything about her, so cooking for her might be tricky. It would be like taking a complete stranger into her home. Bridgette wasn't sure how that would make her feel. Hopefully, she'd feel some sort of bond, the bond of mother and daughter? Could it still be there, after eighteen years of not seeing each other? She would, at last, find out!

CHAPTER 27
THE MEETING

It was a beautiful warm day in August, with a slight breeze and people were without their jackets. Bridgette looked at her watch for the tenth time, and anxiety swept through her body. She'd arrived very early at the railway station and had been waiting for twenty minutes now, which felt like a lifetime. She'd been to the lady's room twice to comb her hair and neaten up her make-up, and was running out of ideas to pass the time.

Fortunately, after having William, she'd regained her figure quite quickly, and today she was wearing a pink flowery scooped neck top and a plain pink skirt. She looked casual but presentable. The pink and white made her look pretty, setting off her dark, shoulder-length hair. She felt sure that she'd recognise her mother. She imagined her to have smart clothes with stylish short blonde hair. But her biggest concern was what Rebecca would think of her. Would she be disappointed? Still, it was far too late to worry now. Today was the day! Whatever happened from now on would have they'd have to learn to accept each other in a totally new way. After so many years it was like starting from the beginning with a biological link.

Bridgette noticed a train slowly pulling into the station on Platform 5. It was a very long train being an express train from London Liverpool Street, and it was on time. It would have to be on time today, wouldn't it? How ironic, she thought. All these years of waiting and the train wasn't even late!

Bridgette glanced quickly from person to person to see if there was a lady of the age and description Rebecca had given on the telephone. The platform was crowded with people. Rebecca told her she'd be wearing a cream jacket and a blue skirt, but it was hard to see anyone who fitted that description when it was so crowded. Then, as the people moved away from the train to meet their friends and family, Bridgette could see a youngish looking woman with short blonde hair wearing a yellow rose clipped to a long cream jacket. She stood out from the crowd. As Bridgette walked on the pathway beside the platform, the woman began to wave. To her surprise, Bridgette lost her inhibitions and waved back enthusiastically. It was undoubtedly her mother because there was something familiar about her which Bridgette couldn't put her finger on.

Rebecca walked towards her, gave her hug and then said hello. Bridgette was amazed that she didn't look the least bit like her, but Rebecca looked exactly as she imagined. Bridgette then noticed that

Rebecca was beaming at her. 'Did you recognise me?' she asked.

'Well, I thought it must be you because most of the people had left and yes you do look familiar,' she replied, cautiously.

'You, look totally different to how I imagined, Bridgette. You must understand that when I left you, you were a tiny baby, so it's hard for me to adjust and think that you're the same person. So many years have passed, and we'll have so much to say to each other,' said Rebecca, with tears in her eyes.

'Yes, and I'm a mother too. I have a lovely partner called Mark.' replied Bridgette, who was also emotional when she spoke about her little family.

'What's the name of your little boy? You didn't say?'

'Oh, he's called William. I named him after a courageous man called William, who was killed during the war. It's a long story that Sister Mary told me.'

'Sister Mary was a very supportive person. At least the Mary, I knew. She tried to take care of everyone and she was always getting into trouble with the Reverend Mother. I don't want to think about that again. Let's concentrate on you. Tell me about your nanny job? That sounds interesting. I'm so happy that you got my letter at last. I wonder what happened to the first one I sent to you. I sent it to your work address, so I don't understand why they didn't forward it.

'Well, that's an extremely long story as well,' replied Bridgette who wondered if they'd thrown away her mail.

'How far is it, to your flat?' asked Rebecca

'Oh, it's not that far, within walking distance. It takes about fifteen minutes. I live near a charming park. I often take William there so that he can let off steam.'

'That sounds lovely. I can't wait to meet William. I keep thinking I'm a grandmother, it's incredible.'

'It is,' replied Bridgette as she wondered how her parents would feel.

'We'll have this morning on our own, then we'll meet Mark. He's going to come home with William late afternoon.'

'Wow, so I will meet both of them! That is wonderful,' exclaimed Rebecca cheerfully.

'Perhaps you might be able to tell me a bit about my father?' asked Bridgette.

'Your father, well, that's difficult, but I'll try.'

Rebecca and Bridgette strolled side by side and quickly fell into step with each other. It was surprising how soon they synchronised, and Bridgette felt there may be other similarities.

As the weeks passed, Bridgette was really pleased she'd traced Rebecca. She was unsure if she would ever be a large part of her life, but they had both said that they wanted to keep in touch by phone and writing. Rebecca had shown Bridgette photographs of her brothers and sisters, her aunt and uncles and their children, her cousins. Most of them lived in Ireland, so there was little chance they'd bump into each other. Bridgette was part of a biological family, and she thought it was strange that she was related to so many people she hadn't met, but this gave her a feeling of stability. Some of her features were similar to those of her aunt and cousins, but she knew nothing of their personalities. Finding her mother had settled some conflict within her. She immediately felt more at ease and she felt a sense of peace.

Bridgette had also been able to tell her parents about meeting Rebecca, and she was surprised at how well they took the news. They were very supportive, and if anything, it made her love them more for being so understanding. She also told them about her meeting with Sister Mary. Bridgette was relieved to discover that her parents were accepting of the situation, but she didn't talk about Neil.

'We always knew that you would want to trace your mother one day,' her mother said.

Bridgette no longer felt guilty. It was great to be able to discuss things openly. Mark was also happy that she got on so well with Rebecca. He was pleased for William.

'You've got another granny now, William. I don't mind if she takes you out as long as I'm still your number one dad!' he said, as he gave Bridgette a friendly wink.

'You're his only dad. You know that. You're really special, and William loves you. Doesn't he always for you when he is crying? He doesn't ask for me! He must know how much you adore him.'

Rebecca was also relieved she'd met Bridgette. Bridgette was a mother and at such a young age. This felt confusing because everything was different from how she imagined. However, she was pleased that the meeting had gone so well, and it was over. Perhaps now, she could get back to her work in the bank and seeing Lawrence. He would be home in a few days, and she couldn't wait. She'd missed him so much. Rebecca knew that things couldn't carry on as they were. She'd have to tell him about the enormous change in her life. She now had a daughter and grandchild. Would Lawrence be able to cope with the news? Whatever happened between them from now on, could be dealt with. Being in touch with her child was important. She'd never had the opportunity to marry or have another child, and now at the age of thirty-nine, she considered it too late. Besides, Lawrence was much older, and he'd never talked of wanting children. He was looking forward to retirement and children weren't part of the plan!

CHAPTER 28
THE UNEXPECTED LETTER

Bridgette felt energised this morning. It was a great autumn day. The sun was shining, and it was still reasonably warm, so she put on her coat and decided to take William to the park. William was just starting to toddle, which was a bit of a nightmare because he wanted to get out of the buggy all the time to try out his new wobbly legs. This was fine in the house in a controlled area where Bridgette could catch him, but some areas of the park weren't suitable for a toddler without proper shoes unless he wanted to get covered in grass and mud.

William was crying and making a huge fuss about being put back in his buggy, so Bridgette did what she swore she'd never do, she gave him his dummy to quieten him down for a short time. They needed a drink and some snacks to take to the park along with bread for the ducks of course! William could manage to throw the ducks food from his pushchair. If it were dry enough, she could take him out for a while!

William needed proper shoes, but money was tight, and they'd spent so much on him already. Mark had learned to be better with money, but it was still tough for them to manage on his earnings alone. She wished that she could do something to help, but at the moment, it was impossible because she needed to be at home for William, so his corduroy padded boots would have to last a little bit longer.

As she opened the front door to take the buggy down the road, the postman handed her a letter. She didn't recognise the handwriting, but she was pleased that it wasn't a bill.

'Thanks,' she said to Tim, who gave her one of his beaming smiles. Bridgette knew that he fancied her because he was always smiling at her from across the road. Sometimes he made little comments asking when she was free. Available, thought Bridgette, those days have definitely gone. Her life was so different now. She quickly opened the letter and discovered it was from Neil, which set her heart pounding. What on earth does he want, after all this time, she thought, feeling slightly stressed.

Dear Bridgette,

I managed to get your forwarding address from Jane who I met bumped into at a conference a few months ago, although I've wanted to contact you for a long time.

Karen and I have split up. She walked out on us a couple of months ago and left me to look after the children. She now lives with a female friend in the city. There was no explanation but I think there must be someone else. Her attitude towards us is unbelievable, she hardly seems the children and it's tough for me to manage on my own. I had a nanny for a few months, but she was useless, and the children didn't like her so I'm now in the terrible position of once again, having to work full time at home. I find it hard to get into the office. It's particularly tricky for me during the school holidays, which are a nightmare.

Jane told me that you wouldn't be interested in becoming a nanny again because you have a baby now and you're too busy. I was shocked to hear this news. Why didn't you get in touch to let us know what was going on? I thought we were friends!

I'm desperate for someone to care for the children who knows them well. Carmel is at school now, so it is mainly after school and during the holidays that I need help. I thought I would get in touch with you on the off chance, you might be interested. I want them to go to school and carry on, as usual, if that's possible!

The children and I really miss you. They kept asking about you for such a long time, and we assumed that you must have another job. Can I meet you and chat over lunch, soon? I can either come to your home, or you could meet me in London if that's easier? If you would prefer to ring, I've left my phone number at the bottom of this letter. I expect you still have our number anyway. I wouldn't bother you with all this, but I need to find a nanny before the children return to school in September. I'm happy for you to bring the baby, which is another thing that we need to talk about!

I hope to hear from you soon.

Love Neil

Bridgette noticed there weren't any kisses on the letter. She was in complete shock that Neil had written to her, so she didn't care! Her first instinct was to throw his letter away, but she couldn't make herself do it! Why was this happening, she thought. Her life had turned into a series of ups and downs! These situations didn't seem to happen to others, or if they did, how on earth did they cope. Was she coping, she wondered as she began to push the pushchair with bold strides towards the park?

Bridgette heard William babbling as if he was singing a happy song which always made her smile, and she reminded herself how lucky she was. Perhaps I just need to talk to someone. Anyone who will help me to straighten a few things out. I never see my friends now, so it will have to be one of my parents. I can't talk to Mark about it all, not yet but perhaps I can talk to Mum or Rebecca? Bridgette didn't know which one of them would be able to cope with this situation, or if either would but she would have to find out!

At last, she plucked up the courage and phoned Rebecca. 'I need to talk to you. I have a problem. I've received a letter from Neil, and he wants to meet me.'

'Neil, from the family you worked for?'

'Yes, that's right. He wants me to go back as a Nanny and look after the children.

'Well, how could he expect you to do that? After all, you've got William and Mark, and then there are your parents. Your life is in Suffolk. You can't leave your responsibilities. What on earth is he thinking about suggesting such a thing?' responded Rebecca angrily.

'There's more to it than that. I'm afraid to tell you this, but William is Neil's child, and I think he knows. I'm worried that he might have some sort of a claim on him.'

'William is Neil's child! You never said anything about that! You really should have been a lot more honest with me, Bridgette. Does Mark know he's isn't the father?'

'Yes, of course, Mark knows, but he doesn't know Neil has contacted me. Oh, what a mess? There are just so many problems. We don't have much money, and things aren't like they were in the beginning. I need to work. I don't want to tell Mark about Neil's letter because it would upset him. I don't know what to do?'

'Do you want to meet Neil because it may be good to get a few things straight.'

'I don't know. I feel it's a bad idea because it'll only cause problems with Mark. I still have feelings for him.''

'Did you love him?' pressed Rebecca.

'Well, I did, and that is why it worries me.'

'Then you do have a problem. We need to talk Bridgette. I'll come and see you, and I'll explain a few things, then perhaps you will understand more about the opposite sex. You need some guidance.'

Rebecca arrived one afternoon in late September, and Bridgette was really pleased to see her. Fortunately, she was coming just after lunch, so they had plenty of time to chat before Mark came home from work.

'That's a bit sudden, isn't it? You've not long met Rebecca, and she's already becoming a frequent visitor,' joked Mark with a smile on his face, which was something Bridgette was used to because Mark took everything in his stride. He didn't read things into situations or misinterpret them. Mark was just Mark. What you saw you got! Bridgette admired this about him, although at times he could also be frustratingly predictable!

Bridgette was relieved that Rebecca was coming to talk. She found it extremely hard not to think about Neil when he sounded so desperate. He must genuinely need help and what about the children? She'd grown fond of them, and it was awful they were in this situation. Why had Karen hardly seen them? What a selfish woman but she had always been wrapped up in her work and excluded the family. Whatever Bridgette did to try and take her mind off Neil, she couldn't stop thinking about him and the times they were together which surprisingly still had an effect on her. What was it about him that did this to her? She kept on picturing his face close to hers as she remembered the first time they kissed in their kitchen when Neil had approached from behind and slid his arms around her. Was she drawn to Neil's element of surprise? Mark was wonderful but they hadn't the same chemistry. She hoped that Rebecca would bring her to her senses because she needed to get on with her life and make the best of it. Unfortunately, it was proving harder than she imagined.

* * * * * * * * * *

The weather had changed, and there was a slight nip in the air as Bridgette set out to meet Rebecca at the station. Her parents were looking after William and Bridgette was surprised how quickly she could walk without a pushchair. The freedom felt great, and Bridgette made a mental note to have these days more often. She would speak to Mark's parents to see if they were willing to look after William a little more. Being a mother was hard, and sometimes suffocating, for a nineteen-year-old. While other girls were out with their friends having fun in pubs and night clubs, she was a full-time mum. Then there were the other pressures. Mark had recently told her they needed to be careful with money. That was fair enough, but William constantly needed things plus he was growing out of his clothes as fast as he got them. Life as a mother was much harder than she'd imagined. She felt isolated from her friends who didn't want to spend any time with her because she was leading a different life. Most of them were at university and still had their parents' support. She had to cope with most things on her own. It was easy for her to think about Neil and the children than to get stuck into thoughts about Mark and money issues. The whole situation was so dull it made her wonder why she'd jumped so quickly back into their relationship. She knew Mark was a fantastic father to William, but it felt as if there was no longer any romance in their relationship. It was all about William, work and money.

Rebecca was already waiting at the station when Bridgette arrived because she was five minutes late.

'I'm sorry, I hurried as fast as I could, but I was late dropping William off to Mum and Dad. I didn't allow enough time to get here.'

'That's all right, I knew you were coming. Let's go and have a coffee and perhaps a sandwich in town. Then we can have a proper chat. I'm starving. I didn't have any lunch on the train because it was expensive.'

Bridgette took Rebecca to a charming little café, over a health food shop in the local town. It was always packed at lunchtime, but by mid-afternoon, it was quite empty. They more or less had the place to themselves, which was better for talking. They sat on a table that overlooked the town. They could see people busily shopping in the street below. The café was specialised in vegetarian food and healthy eating. Rebecca's was really pleased with the menu because she liked to eat as healthily as possible.

'Let it be my treat. It must be hard being on one salary with a baby,' said Rebecca.

'Thank you,' replied Bridgette.

'So, tell me right from the beginning, what happened with Neil and why would he bother contacting you after all this time?'

Bridgette felt that talking to Rebecca was more like talking to an older sister, than a mother, and talking about Neil was fairly easy. When she finally finished, she turned to observe her reaction.

'Men are hard to rely on,' started Rebecca. 'I was in love with your father, but he too was married. He promised me the world. He even said he'd leave his wife, who he said he no longer loved. I soon fell into the trap of believing whatever he said. I suppose it was naivety on my part, but I was looking for love and security. I liked the feeling of an older man looking after me, especially one who was wealthy and powerful. I managed to keep our meetings secret from everybody until I fell pregnant. When I told Michael about my pregnancy, he didn't want to know. He said that the baby wasn't his, what did I expect him to do about it. My whole life was in ruins, and I didn't know what to do. I wanted to keep you, Bridgette, you must believe me, I really wanted to, but I had no choice. I had no friends, no support and very little money. I couldn't return to my family. They would never have accepted me back in that condition. That's why I had to go to St. Catherine's.''

Rebecca hastily wiped tears from her eyes with a handkerchief, and Bridgette felt a strong desire to put her arms around Rebecca and comfort her, but for some reason, she was unable to because her life was in a mess, she had nothing to give.

'I'm telling you this, Bridgette, in the hope that you'll understand. You've found someone who really cares for you. You're lucky. I didn't find Lawrence until much later on, and I was never fortunate enough to have another child. Mark loves you and William, and that's something special. It is also and something worth hanging on to. Please don't do as I did and put all your hopes and dreams on an older man because he appears to offer you something better. You're attracted to him, which isn't the same as love, and it won't last. What will you do then, who will want you with a small child?'

Bridgette was quiet for a long time. She was right. What had happened with Neil was in the past, and he only wanted her to look after his children. She had William now, and his future was vital to her. She didn't want William to be without a father or to be stuck in some flat on her own if things didn't work out. She knew that her feelings for Neil were purely physical. He was a handsome and charming man who could persuade any young lady into doing what he wanted, including going to bed. She wasn't going to fall into that trap again. She'd phone him and say she was sorry but she had her own life now. She had to put Mark and William first, and that would be the end of it all. Mark wasn't perfect, but at least he was reliable.

'I'll tell him no,' she replied.

'That's the spirit. That is much more like my daughter. I can see that you also have my determination and will to succeed. Thank goodness for that.'

The rest of the weekend with Rebecca went well. Mark took them out to the seaside on Sunday for a walk along the seafront. The coast was about fifteen miles away, and they didn't often go because of the cost of petrol, but today was a special occasion being Mark's birthday. They walked along the seafront, looking at the huge ships on the horizon, while eating fish and chips. There was quite a sea breeze, but it was still enjoyable. The sun sparkled on top of the water which reminded Bridgette of some of Neil's paintings, particularly of the fishing boats which he had painted in oils. As they sat on the wooden beach to eat, William kicked his legs rhythmically in the pushchair, and grinned under a large floppy sun hat. He looked great in a brand-new outfit that Rebecca had bought especially for today. They soon discovered how much William enjoyed chips as he grasped large handfuls and squashed them into his mouth!

Bridgette felt relaxed with Rebecca. She was relieved that things were, at last, going to be okay.

CHAPTER 29
NEIL

It was eight-thirty, and Bridgette had overslept. She was awoken by the slam of the front door which meant Mark had just left for work. There was no sound from William's cot. He must be exhausted after such a busy weekend, thought Bridgette as she slowly emerged from bed.

Rebecca had gone back to London late last night because she had to return to work this morning. Mark had got up early to get his own breakfast so Bridgette could have a lay in which she considered thoughtful. She went to turn on the shower and take a peek at William, who still appeared to be sleeping soundly. Bridgette was pleased he was quiet because it gave her the chance to have a proper shower and wash her hair before breakfast. She'd been in the shower about ten minutes when there was suddenly a loud banging on the front door. She wanted to ignore it because it was most likely the postman bringing a parcel, but as it continued, she reluctantly grabbed a towel and held it around her. She cautiously opened the door a couple of inches and then jumped back in horror, nearly losing the towel!

'Oh, my goodness, Neil,' she exclaimed.

'Hello Bridgette, I didn't receive a reply to my letter, or my invitation to lunch, so I decided to visit you to ask you in person! Actually, I'm working in the area all this week doing some valuation work, so I had to see you being so close,' explained Neil.

Bridgette found it hard to take in. She was also conscious of how she looked with a towel draped around her with dripping wet hair.

'I'm sorry if I've shocked you. I wish that I'd phoned now,' Neil continued.

'Come in then. It's a shock, but if you want to, you can wait in the kitchen while I get dressed and get William up. He should have had his breakfast by now, but he' sleeping like an angel. This will put him out of his routine.'

Bridgette showed Neil to the kitchen and filled up the kettle, then left him to make coffee. Half an hour later, she appeared dressed in a casual pair of jeans and a low-necked tee shirt. When Bridgette had finished making William's breakfast, and he was happily feeding himself in his highchair, she sat down to talk to Neil.

'So, this is the little guy that I've waited so long to meet? He looks just like his mum! Bridgette, I want you to come back and live with us. We all miss you, and I've thought about you so much since you left us. I wondered for ages why you never returned in January, then, I gradually put two and two together. It became obvious why you were unwell in those last few weeks. What I don't understand is why you didn't talk to me about it, unless you deliberately wanted to hide something. Is William my child?' asked Neil, suddenly demanding the truth.

Bridgette was horrified. She didn't know how to react. Neil had discovered the truth, and by the look on his face, he wasn't going to let it go! She felt utterly backed up a corner and realised that he could easily manipulate her because there was no doubt that if she admitted he was the father, he'd have some rights of access to William. This was going to be difficult for all of them especially Mark! Why, oh why, did she answer the door to him. If she denied the truth, things could get very unpleasant and Mark knew the truth already, so there was no choice but to be honest. After a few minutes of silence, Bridgette spoke with some hesitancy.

'William is your child, you're right. That means his biological father, but Mark has looked after William since birth. He supported me throughout my pregnancy, so he looks upon Mark as his dad. He's done everything for him. It would be really confusing for William to suddenly have another father in his life. Besides, Mark is totally besotted with William, and it would be unfair to change things', said Bridgette as forcefully as she could. Neil looked at her and decided to continue his own story.

'To be honest, a few months ago I met up with your friend Jane at a conference we both attended. In fact, I've seen her several times because she works for a large London insurance company that we partner with. She gave me the impression that you were miserable and felt trapped, that's partly why I came to see you, Bridgette. I want you to come home where you belong so we can bring up our son. I want our family to be together. I haven't told the children yet, but I want to. Karen has someone else and she isn't coming back. The children are accepting it now, not that I ever really will. The kids need someone in their lives who they know and trust, and I need a person who I can rely on so that I can work and pay the bills. I promise you, Bridgette, that you'll have a far better life with me than stuck in this flat. You'll never have to worry about money. Mark is obviously special to you, I understand that, but I get the feeling you don't love him. He'll never be able to support you the way I can,' replied Neil, who was clearly not giving up.

Bridgette realised that she was getting way out of her depth. She didn't want this man interfering in her life, yet there were a lot of truths in what he said. Being in the flat all day on her own while Mark was at work, wasn't the life she imagined, it was lonely. She couldn't go out and spend money because things were tight and William would go without things he needed. As for herself, new clothes were a thing of the past, she was beginning to look as if she was dressed from a jumble sale which was damaging her self-esteem. Could Neil give her a better life and would the children accept them as a couple? Or did he intend her to be their nanny as before? Would William be recognised as the children's brother, or her child? She found it very confusing. As if from nowhere, Neil's hand gently slid on top hers, and he squeezed it to reassure her.

'I know it's a lot for you to take in Bridgette, but think about it. You know that I can give you a better life and besides I've always thought we have a special connection and now I understand why, we have little William. He is absolutely great. I can't believe it. I can't understand why I haven't been to see him until now. Although it wasn't until recently, when I met up with Jane, that I realised I couldn't leave it any longer. She explained what has been going on since you left us. As soon as I found out, I came to see you.'

'Neil, please stop. I'm so confused. You are right, I don't know how I feel about Mark anymore, and I don't know how I feel about the things you mentioned. I need some time to think. I'm really fine as I am. I know Mark isn't perfect and we don't have much money, but surely money isn't everything? William is loved, and this is his home, so I don't know whether I want to change things not now anyway.'

'Bridgette,' he said, pulling her to her feet to draw her close. 'Don't you miss me? You must remember what it was like between us. I certainly do,' replied Neil as he breathed into her ear. 'It isn't something that's easily forgotten. I never had those feelings for Karen.'

Bridgette's heart almost skipped a beat. How could she forget the sexual feelings she had for this man and now they were returning?

'I can't make any promises, but I'll think about it,' she murmured.

Neil played with William for another half an hour, and decided not to put any more pressure on Bridgette. To her surprise, he then gave her a quick peck on the cheek and walked over to the door, saying that he'd be in touch in a few days.

Bridgette was relieved. Perhaps now things could return to normal, but she knew that Neil would want an answer soon because the summer was nearly over.

CHAPTER 30
CHOICES

'You saw him?' asked Rebecca

'Yes, I didn't have a choice, he arrived on the doorstep, so I let him in so we could talk.'

'I suppose he offered you the world?'

'Well nearly,' whispered Bridgette.

'He offered you your old job back and more money to help with William. He'll never accept you as a proper member of his family, Bridgette. Men like him don't.'

'Yes, he will. William is his son, and he wants us both.'

'He just wants you back for convenience until he finds his next victim and then you'll be out again, and Mark will be gone.'

'It might be a risk I have to take.'

'You're a silly girl. I told you to put him straight.'

'I can do what I like. You're not my mother.' Bridgette shouted.

There was a long silence from Rebecca.

'Go and ask your mother then, and see what she makes of it all. I'll tell you something now, she'll say exactly the same as me. Anyway, I warned you. I don't want to be involved with this anymore because it's causing me too much aggravation, after all I've got Lawrence coming back shortly. I don't want him to see me stressed out. I've had enough ups and downs in my life without all this. I'm sorry, but you've made your bed so you'll have to lay in it. Please don't contact me again because I can't support you. I enjoyed meeting you and William, but as far as I can see, you're throwing everything good in your life away!'

Bridgette started to cry. Why was Rebecca behaving like this? Had she said too much? Life was hard enough as it was. Surely, she could share her feelings, if not, what was their relationship about? It wasn't as if Rebecca had told her not to talk about it because she had offered to come over to discuss it and now, she wanted to disappear from her life! Tears streamed down Bridgette's face. She'd made a mistake seeing Neil again. Although, he was right about one thing; she didn't love Mark because all she thought about was him! His beautiful house, his children and the times they were together. Part of her wanted to accept Neil's offer to get out of their pokey flat. Surely it would be better for William? Rebecca's opinion had annoyed her. She didn't want to lose her relationship with her, but it felt like it was already over. She was unwilling to support her. What did she know anyway, when she was the woman who gave her away to make her life easier! Had it been unwise to trace her when she had so little understanding? Who could she turn to now? It was impossible to talk to Mark, that would be too painful.

The time would come for that, but first, her parents had to know about Neil. She'd have to explain the truth about him being William's father which wasn't going to be easy!

* * * * * * * * *

'Mum, I've been stupid,' said Bridgette, a few days later.

'Bridgette, what on earth is the matter? You have looked a little unhappy lately, but I put that down to a few money problems. Is there something you're not telling me?'

It was Thursday morning and a good day to talk because Mark was at work. Bridgette had walked to her parents' house and found her mother alone because her father had gone shopping. She didn't feel like going through everything again because it was such a long story so she decided to keep things simple and leave out some of the detail. When Bridgette finally paused for breath, she was pleasantly surprised by how well her mother listened. There was no judgement about what had happened with Neil and she appeared quite understanding.

After a very long silence, her mother said, 'Well, you've been keeping all sorts of things from me, haven't you? Why on earth didn't you come to me before because there aren't any problems which we can't sort out together. Although it sometimes takes a while to know where your loyalties lie. I tend to agree with Rebecca I'm afraid, I think that this Neil wants to use you to look after the children. He's obviously in a bit of hole. You say you're not sure if you love Mark, but Neil isn't the answer to your problems, beware of men wearing masks.'

'Men wearing masks?' asked Bridgette, who felt a little bewildered.

'Yes, people who aren't the person they appear to be. They put on a mask to the world, which is a face people see, and everyone believes they are nice, but underneath it's all pretence!'

'You mean they're nothing special?' asked Bridgette in a curious way. 'Like wearing an actor's mask?'

'Yes, a bit like that! Remember, Bridgette that surface things have no depth to them. If there are no foundations, there is nothing to build on. They may appear to be fine and well-polished, but they create an illusion. What can appear beautiful is merely skin deep,' said her mother with a sigh.

'When we adopted you, you were beautiful, and you still are. We love you because you are our Bridgette and we are not putting any expectations on you. That's what's great about your relationship with Mark. He loves William as his child. He also loves you too, for who you are. It doesn't worry him that he isn't William's father. He sees everything William does as a gift.'

Bridgette walked over to the mirror that stood in her parent's hallway. She loved that mirror. It was the place where Bridgette had combed her hair while living at home. She stared at her own reflection and looked deep into her eyes. Perhaps I need to grow up and appreciate what Mark does for me. I also need to realise how special William is, instead of thinking about me all the time, she thought.

'I love you Mum, and you've really helped. A mother is someone who teaches you the valuable things in life,' said Bridgette giving her a hug.

'I'm always here for you. You only have to ask.'

Bridgette went home later that afternoon. She now knew what her answer was going to be to Neil. As Bridgette walked along the road, with William babbling away in his pushchair, she saw Mark arriving home from work in his car and wondered why he was home early.

'Bridgette, come quickly, I've got a surprise.'

Bridgette rushed into the house, took off her coat and unclipped William from his pushchair. She hoped the news would be good because she had had enough of disappointments!

'Guess what? I've got a promotion at work to the head of design, which means a significant pay rise plus a company car and I've also got another surprise. I want you to marry me. Now, is as good a time as any. I don't want us to wait! I would have asked you a long time ago, but I wanted us to be able to afford to do things properly, a nice wedding and a honeymoon. What do you think, Bridgette? Will you marry me?' Mark asked eagerly.

Marks' words came as a massive shock to her. She didn't know what to say. She was unsure. Seeing

Neil had brought up feelings which she'd forgotten. Now, she was faced with a tough choice. She knew that Mark was reliable and dependable, but something was missing. She also thought about how Rebecca had reacted when she'd told her about Neil and also about her Mum's words. Her mother was understanding, even if Rebecca wasn't, but at the same time, it was evident that they both thought Neil was playing some kind of game. Perhaps he was only thinking of him. She knew that Mark would stand by her through thick and thin, and they could have a good life together. Life was not just about money, there was also trust. It wasn't as if it was all about her either because she had to think about what was best for William.

She looked at Mark, who was obviously waiting patiently for her answer. He was now down on one knee!

'Please, get up, Mark! The truth is, it's got nothing to do with Neil, or anyone else, but I'm not sure if I want to be married,' she answered boldly. "Why don't we keep things as they are for now? I need a little time to think.'

Bridgette walked out into the garden and looked up at the sun. It was hiding behind the clouds. Soon they would pass, and the sun would set majestically on the horizon. Nothing was more powerful than the sun before it went down, nor more beautiful. She took a long deep breath. She could watch the sky for hours, but Mark deserved some sort of an answer.

When the sun has gone, she said to herself as she watched it disappear into a gorgeous glow.

As Bridgette walked back into the house, she suddenly realised she didn't have to make a decision at all. When and if she made one, she would no longer be influenced by other's opinions because her own choices gave her identity. They formed a map or root. Bridgette knew that her journey over the last few years had finally given her something that she'd been looking for. She was suddenly engulfed by a newfound feeling of confidence and security.

Mark stayed downstairs, but Bridgette was so tired that she went up to bed. As she cast her eye around their bedroom, she suddenly noticed the little blue bible that had been given to her by Sister Mary. It was strange to have never opened it, but she suddenly felt the time was right. Perhaps there were words within its pages which would help her. She opened the front cover and was surprised to see an inscription written in italics.

> Beautiful Mary,
> You are always with me. Please wait for me, my, soon to be, wife.
> Love and blessings
> William - 14th February 1940

Bridgette was stunned. The Bible had been in her possession since she was first pregnant, with William, yet she had never opened the cover to read it. Imagine Sister Mary giving her such a beautiful and treasured gift and why? Perhaps, she no longer wanted it, or maybe it was too painful to hold on to any longer. Bridgette decided to flick through the rest of it. To her utter amazement, she discovered that a huge hole was cut out of the centre of the bible. There were no more pages, just a deep hole which appeared to be stuffed with some brown tissue paper which could have initially been white. Bridgette gently tugged at the wrapping, and the small bundle dropped out on to her bed. She slowly opened it up, and there on her bed was the most incredibly beautiful engagement ring, its blue sapphires, and diamonds sparkled like new.

Bridgette gasped. She simply didn't know what to do. Her first instinct was to shout to Mark, but instead, Bridgette turned the ring around in her hand for several minutes, staring at it in amazement. Then, she bravely slipped it on to her wedding finger. Bridgette had long slim fingers and rings seldom fitted, but remarkedly the ring fitted her perfectly. She closed the Bible and carefully replaced it on the shelf. Her heart was thumping. It felt as if she had gone back in time. It was an extraordinary experience and something that she wouldn't forget. Sister Mary, you are a treasure, Rebecca was right!

'William, you have made this woman extremely happy. I will marry you!' she said out loud, laughing with sheer joy and excitement.

Bridgette ran downstairs to find Mark, who was now nearly asleep in the chair. She knew that he wouldn't attempt to come to bed because he wanted to give her some space so she shook him gently.

'Wake up, wake up. Mark. I've got something to tell you. You won't believe this. Look we're engaged!

CHAPTER 31
SISTER MARY'S GARDEN

Sister Mary walked around her tiny garden. It had been a year since she'd left St. Catherine's, and she felt happy. Her roses were beautiful. She particularly liked the yellow ones with beautiful blooms. There was also a deep red rose which only had three flowers, but the shade reminded her of a rose that she'd received from William many years ago.

Her work in the community was much lighter, and her sciatica had started to ease. She had many meetings with various groups who said they were willing to support St. Catherine's and Mary had been successful in acquiring some much-needed funding. Things were changing because there were no new babies for adoption and instead of St. Catherine's closing, it was being transformed into a rest home where nuns could come and have a few weeks respite. The building was going to be updated if they received enough funding from the local community, and the church. Mary was positive the transition would take place because she'd already started to make good headway with the project.

It was nearly ten o'clock, and Mary suddenly heard a knock on her door. She quickly walked across her garden and noticed the postman standing there.

'Ah, there are you, Mary, I've got some post for you. I gave it to the sister at the main building, but she insisted I bring it to you at the cottage,' said the postman.

Mary said 'thank you,' and took what appeared to be a personally written letter to her, from the postman. She could hardly believe that someone had written to her because apart from the odd Christmas card, it was rare. Mary walked into her tiny kitchen and put her kettle on to make a pot of tea. When it had boiled, she sat down and opened the letter. She looked at the signature, and saw it was from Bridgette Woods. It felt like a long time ago since they'd met, but Mary remembered Bridgette was a charming girl.

Dear Mary

I'm writing to thank you for all the help you gave me in reuniting me with my birth mother Rebecca. We had a meeting several months ago and we are now getting to know each other. I also wanted to let you that Mark and I are now engaged. We'd like to invite you to our wedding next year because I feel that it is due to your help that we got back together! I decided to name our little boy William, after your

William, and would you believe it, he's now one years old!

I'm wearing the ring that fell out of the bible you gave me when I visited you. I feel William must have been an exceptional person to have given you such a beautiful ring. I'm so grateful, and Mark loves it. It was such a surprise. A message from God!

I've enclosed some photographs of William in the garden of our new house. We lived in a flat first, but it was cramped with all his toys! Fortunately, Mark has a new job, and we have a lot more space plus I am thinking about going back to work part-time. Please let us know if you can come to our wedding nearer the time because it isn't until August next year and it's in Suffolk. I hope you can manage to get here.

Hoping you are well and enjoying your retirement!

Best Wishes
Bridgette Woods

Sister Mary folded the letter and looked at the photographs of William. He had beautiful blonde wavy hair and looked healthy. What a delightful child, she thought. There was also a picture of Mark and William together sitting on the beach. William had a bucket and spade in his hand. She couldn't quite remember the story now but was it something about Bridgette being pregnant by her employer. Had she been a Nanny? It was hard to believe that Mark wasn't William's father when he looked so much like him. Incredible she thought, folding up the letter.

Mary re-filled her cup with a little more tea. Fortunately, she had plenty of time today, so she could finish her painting later this afternoon. Mary was making good progress with watercolours, but needed to be careful not to spill water on her lovely table like last time! As she spread out a pile of magazines which she had picked up from the waiting room at St. Catherine's, she suddenly noticed a sizeable bold advertisement for a cosmetics company called Super Glow. Mary was immediately drawn to the ad. Wasn't that company mentioned in the letters, the one Gillian started? How could it be? Was it just a cruel coincidence? Mary looked at the advertisement again.

SUPER GLOW

'A natural change for evolving women.'

Mary quickly turned the page, only to discover a full feature about a lady called Gillian who started a hugely successful company in Colorado which had now spread into Europe. She was soon to be launching products in England. Mary scanned the article in total disbelief. It told the story of how quickly her business had grown and how the products had recently been adapted to include more natural ingredients.

Mary's eyes quickly went to the picture of the woman in the article. She was lovely. Her skin was glowing, and her eyes shone. Her shiny hair which was dark brown bobbed on her shoulders in a fashionable style. Could this be Gillian? Her Gillian, the lady who was mentioned in the letters, it didn't seem possible. Was there a resemblance between this beautiful young woman and herself? Mary continued to read finish the article. The British range was coming out in the Spring and Gillian said it was to be called 'April.'

Tears flowed down Mary's face as she stared in astonishment. She still had the box of letters that had convinced her Gillian was her daughter. 'When April arrives, it will be a breath of fresh air she whispered,' remembering the words in the letter.

Mary stood in front of the mirror and looked closely at herself. She then removed her veil and brushed her hair. 'God works in mysterious ways,' she said,' and took out her pen and paper.

ABOUT THE AUTHOR

Jennifer Lynch lives in Norfolk. She's a keen walker, animal lover and dancer. She started writing to keep her busy in the evenings when she was a single parent and didn't have a life!

She now works as an empowerment coach and reiki healer, writer and poet.

Her books include The Silver Lining, William's Wishes, Liberty Angel, Never to be Told, Salsa, We Hear You Angels and the eBooks 5th Dimensional Earth and Attracting What You Really Want.

She can be contacted via her website www.angelwisdom.co.uk

Printed in Great Britain
by Amazon